Ann McIntosh w[illegible]
frozen north for a [illegible] resides in
sunny central Flor[illegible] husband. She's a proud
mama to three grown children, loves tea, crafting,
animals (except reptiles!), bacon and the ocean. She
believes in the power of romance to heal, inspire and
provide hope in our complex world.

The Nurse's Pregnancy Miracle
is **Ann McIntosh**'s debut title

Look out for more books from Ann McIntosh
Coming soon

Discover more at millsandboon.co.uk.

THE NURSE'S PREGNANCY MIRACLE

ANN McINTOSH

MILLS & BOON

Published in Great Britain 2018
by Mills & Boon, an imprint of HarperCollins*Publishers*
1 London Bridge Street, London, SE1 9GF

ISBN: 978-0-263-93372-7

MIX
Paper from
responsible sources
FSC® C007454

This book is produced from independently certified FSC™ paper
to ensure responsible forest management.
For more information visit www.harpercollins.co.uk/green.

Printed and bound in Spain
by CPI, Barcelona

This book is dedicated to my late mother, Helen Delvaillé,
a voracious Harlequin/Mills & Boon reader.
I think she'd be happy to see my book
printed by her favourite publisher,
although she'd probably just deadpan, 'Oh, good.'
Not all romantics are effusive!

CHAPTER ONE

WALKING BRISKLY THROUGH the waiting area of the Lauderlakes Family Medical Center, Nychelle Cory scanned the room, once more noting the contrast between the opulent surroundings and the rather squalid interior of the inner-city clinic she'd worked at up until just a couple of years before.

The marble flooring and the crystal chandelier, hung precisely beneath the domed skylight, wouldn't be out of place in a grand home. Instead of the standard faux leather seating typical of medical clinics, comfortable upholstered chairs and love seats were arranged in small clusters around antique side tables. Every inch of the place was designed to give the illusion of being a luxurious hotel lobby, perhaps in the hope of helping people forget they were waiting to see a doctor.

Few people would understand but, oh, how she missed the hustle and near chaos of working at the low-cost clinic. So rewarding, helping those that others often forgot. But she'd known from the moment she took the job there that, financially, it wouldn't be enough to advance *The Plan*.

Funny to realize that was how she always thought of it—not as Plan A, or as a prospective life plan. Just *The Plan*, with caps and italics, the way she'd written it in her diary when she was just thirteen years old. Below that she'd listed what she wanted, and the list was pretty short.

Children. Three or four.
A job that lets me spend lots of time with them.
A nice husband who wants to spend time with the kids too.

Looking back on it, number three had been tacked on at the end, as if she'd already made up her mind that the husband wasn't exactly a necessary part of the process.

That thought made her suppress a little snort of laughter. *The Plan* definitely hadn't come about the way she'd initially thought it would, but she wasn't complaining. In fact she'd go so far as to claim she had the best of all worlds.

Getting a plum job at Fort Lauderdale's premier general care clinic was helping bring her dreams to fruition, yet money alone wouldn't have lured her to Lauderlakes. Her need to help the less fortunate was strong, and luckily Dr. Hamatty, Lauderlakes' founder, believed in giving back too, working with local charities to put on free clinics three times a year.

Not the same as being in the trenches all the time, but it helped give her altruistic nature much-needed satisfaction.

There were a handful of people scattered around the waiting area. Sitting close together on a love seat, phones in hand, were a young couple who looked as though they'd just stepped out from between the pages of a high-end travel magazine. In the play area, just visible behind a floor-to-ceiling, glass-paneled waterfall, a toddler laughed, the sound muted by the tinkle of water.

Nodding hello to her next patient—a stylish older lady seated in a club chair—Nychelle paused for a moment in front of the intake desk and transferred her attention to Gina, the receptionist, who gave one of her usual tight-lipped smiles.

"Glad to see you back." Gina raised one perfectly groomed brow as she spoke quietly, the way they were all instructed to, so as to maintain the atmosphere. "Did you have a good vacation?"

"I wouldn't call it a vacation." Nychelle gave a quick shrug, even as her heart did that trip-hammer thing it kept doing every time she thought about her days off and what they could mean. "Just took some time to get some things done."

Like undergo intrauterine insemination and then keep quiet for a few days to give my body the best chance to make a baby.

Thankfully her complexion was too dark to show the blush as heat rushed up from the neck of her silk shirt and the stylish lab coat covering it into her face. Keeping her expression neutral was so hard, but imperative. Despite Gina's chic, cool appearance, the receptionist was a Class A gossip, highly effective in ferreting out any and all information others tried to keep from her. With just the slightest hint of anything out of the ordinary going on Gina would be off and running.

"Boring." Gina drew the softly spoken word out until it was half a mile long, flipping a long curl of black hair over her shoulder for emphasis. "I was at the very least hoping to hear you'd gone to Jamaica." The smile was a little more relaxed, a little more interrogatory. "The stories I've heard about your homeland and the men there…"

Nychelle couldn't hold back a little gurgle of laughter as she took another look at the information on the tablet in her hand.

Katalina Ivanenko.
Sixty-two years old.
Routine wellness check, including follow-up on previous bone density test.
History of arthritis…

"The rumors of my countrymen's decadence are highly exaggerated." Then she couldn't resist winking and adding a whispered, "Most of the time."

When Gina hid a giggle behind her hand, a little spurt of relief at pulling the wool over the other woman's eyes made Nychelle's smile widen.

No one, with the exception of her cousin and best friend, Aliya, would know about the IUI before her pregnancy was a *fait accompli.* Most people wouldn't get why, at just twenty-eight, she was going this route. They'd expect her to be dating, looking for a long-term relationship, as though she should and would want that. *Nope.* Not in the cards. The relationship she'd gotten out of two years before had shattered both her faith in her own instincts and her ability to trust any man's intentions.

Then there were her medical issues, which would only make conception harder the longer she waited to try. This was the optimal time for her to get pregnant, while leaving herself room to try a few more times if she needed to, and she was grabbing the opportunity with both hands. It was what she'd planned and worked toward since Nick had dumped her, and she knew she was extremely lucky to be able, both emotionally and financially, to make this huge step alone.

The reception phone rang, distracting Gina, and Nychelle took the opportunity to turn away toward her patient.

"Oh!"

The sound was so unexpectedly loud in the hushed environment, so rife with pain and surprise, Nychelle instinctively turned toward its source.

The young woman on the love seat was bent over, in obvious distress, her hands pressed to her lower abdomen.

"Call Dr. Leeson." Nychelle was already moving across the waiting area toward the couple as she threw the demand back over her shoulder to Gina.

"It's okay, Gina. I've got it."

The deep voice came from near the door leading to the clinic, and by the time Nychelle had stooped down beside the young woman Dr. David Warmington was coming up behind her.

Great.

No time to dwell on how unsettled Dr. Warmington made her, or to wonder if he was the right physician for the situation. The other nurses said his bedside manner was exemplary, in between singing his praises and panting over the man's incredible good looks.

"He's not bringing the warm," Nancy, the nursing coordinator, had said with a laugh before he'd started. "He's packing heat."

Among the nurses the name stuck, and to hear them talk you'd think "Dr. Heat" was more enticing than free chocolate and a bottle of Chablis.

Secretly Nychelle agreed, but nothing would get her to admit it. She knew all too well the danger of handsome men—espccially those able to somehow charm even the most hardened of nurses. They weren't to be trusted, and were apt to use their looks to their own advantage and the disadvantage of others.

No doubt if he wanted to he could make a lot of money modeling, showcasing expensive sunglasses on that chiseled face, with the wind blowing through his toffee-colored hair. Or making women run out to buy cologne in the hopes of suddenly transforming their hubbies into a six-foot, two-inch wall of muscle, with linebacker shoulders and a bootie made for nipping.

One glance from his intent blue eyes, reminiscent of the most gorgeous of Florida skies, could make the coldest heart quicken—even hers. But, while Nychelle admired his looks, she viewed him with suspicion—as she now did most, if not all, men.

Pushing all those thoughts aside, she said to the young woman, "Hi, I'm Nychelle. Tell me what's going on."

She took the other woman's wrist firmly between her fingers, finding a strong but rapid pulse, and noting the patient's pallor and the perspiration dotting her hairline despite the clamminess of her skin.

"I… I'm pregnant. I just realized a day ago. I was going to see my doctor after I got home."

A visitor to the area, then, with perfect but accented English. Wide brown eyes, gleaming with tears, looked beseechingly into Nychelle's, as though hoping for an instant end to fear and pain. Then she doubled over with a little shriek, arms crossed protectively over her abdomen.

Hugging her, the man beside her interjected, "She did a home test, but we knew she was not far along. When my wife saw a little blood and was worried, my *tio* told us to come here—"

The young woman turned toward her husband and unleashed a spate of angry, rapid-fire words. Working in Florida, Nychelle had made sure to keep up with her Spanish, but now she caught only the occasional familiar-sounding word. Something about a boat trip, his uncle, and losing her baby, in what Nychelle assumed was Portuguese.

"No, no. Don't worry about any of that now." Sympathetic but firm, the doctor's voice cut through the young woman's tirade and drew the couple's attention. "I'm Dr. Warmington. Come with me and let's find out what's happening, okay?"

Nychelle was watching the patient and saw the moment when, even through her pain, the woman registered how handsome the doctor was. The young woman's eyes widened and her lips parted on a silent *Oh*.

Under different circumstances it would have made Nychelle want to giggle, but they were already moving, the patient supported by her husband on one side, the doctor on the other, through Reception toward the examination rooms.

Nychelle simultaneously held doors open and pulled up the young woman's information on her tablet, in preparation for handing it to Dr. Warmington on arrival at their destination.

Not a miscarriage. Please, not a miscarriage.

The thought caught her by surprise, made her stomach clench and roll, and as she began helping Mrs. Cardozo undress, she realized her hands were shaky.

Steady. Steady.

She was projecting. She knew she was. Imagining herself in Mrs. Cardozo's position, feeling the other woman's emotions as if they were her own, instead of putting her mind where it needed to be—on the equipment Dr. Warmington would need, the tests he'd want her to run.

It was the first time in her career she'd ever felt this way while in the midst of an emergency. Usually if she fell apart it was afterward, when she was alone and could release her emotions in private.

Taking a deep breath, and then another, she forced back all the fears building in her mind, and by the time she'd helped Mrs. Cardozo onto the examination table she'd gotten herself together.

"We're ready for you, Dr. Warmington."

Habitual efficiency took over then, and the well-remembered routine of working with a doctor kicked in—although since qualifying as an Advanced Practice Registered Nurse she usually worked alone, or with her own nurse assistant.

Yet her emotions seemed perilously close to the surface, and it was only Dr. Warmington's soothing presence that kept her on an even keel. On the few occasions she'd witnessed him with patients before she'd been impressed by his professional demeanor, but this was different. Even though his understanding and reassurance were aimed at the patient, Nychelle found herself reacting to it too, letting it wash over her in calming waves.

"I can confirm you're pregnant."

Nychelle noted that he spoke to Mrs. Cardozo, rather than to her husband the way some other male physicians would be inclined to—another point in the doctor's favor.

"But," he continued, "I can see no apparent reason for the symptoms you're experiencing."

He glanced at Mr. Cardozo for a moment, and Nychelle thought his gaze briefly dropped to where the young couple's fingers were tightly intertwined.

"It could be something as simple as dehydration, or a complication that will only become apparent with further testing, so I recommend you go to Broward Medical and have an obstetrician take a look at you there. While we have our own specialists here, at the hospital they'd be able to deal with any eventuality."

As he gave them the information for the hospital, Nychelle slipped into the adjoining office to call ahead and make arrangements. The entire situation had taken maybe thirty minutes, but she felt as though it had been an emotionally grueling marathon. She didn't even realize her eyes were damp until she reached up to swipe at a tear.

Hanging up the phone, she stiffened her spine and turned to find Dr. Warmington watching her from the doorway. Perhaps it was the set of his lips, or the way he seemed to be watching her, with a hint of the gentleness he'd lavished on Mrs. Cardozo, but whatever it was made Nychelle's heart rate escalate and warmth bloom in her chest.

Once more thankful for the cocoa-toned skin that made her blushes unnoticeable, she said the first thing that came to her mind. "You speak Portuguese?"

He laughed quietly as he stepped into his office and moved toward the desk. "I'm lucky to have an ear for languages. I speak a few and understand a few more."

"Lucky indeed."

She should go. Although another nurse practitioner would have seen the patient she'd left waiting in the reception area, the day's schedule was full. No doubt there was another patient for her to see. And she had details to iron out regarding the free child wellness clinic she was helping coordinate, scheduled for the coming weekend. Yet she lingered, watching as Dr. Warmington sat down and pulled his chair up to the desk.

"I'm pretty good with Spanish," she said, after a moment, "but never got past that. Out of curiosity, what was Mrs. Cardozo saying to her husband?"

When he looked up, Nychelle's breath caught in her throat. For an infinitesimal moment she read excruciating hurt in his eyes, but then he blinked and it was gone.

"They're here from Sao Paulo, visiting his uncle, and when she realized she was pregnant she didn't want to go on the boat trip they'd planned. But her husband talked her into it. She was saying if she lost the baby she'd never forgive him."

He was still looking at her, seemingly waiting for her to reply, and suddenly—desperately—she wanted to say the right thing; wished she knew what the right response was. Wished she could smile and soothe the hurt she was sure she'd seen in his eyes.

"Well," she said slowly. "That was patently unfair, but pregnant women—especially those expecting their first child—aren't always known for their rationality."

She risked a little smile, and was relieved and unreasonably happy when those stern lips relaxed into an answering tilt: not quite a smile, but enough.

"Hormones running rampant, as you men are quick to point out."

That brought a wider smile, and Nychelle laughed quietly, before turning away from the magnetic pull of his grin.

"I won't tell anyone you said something so blatantly sexist, Nurse Cory. It'll be our secret."

The laughter in his voice lightened her mood more, even as the rich baritone trickled like liquid sin down her spine. Suddenly she was glad she didn't have to work with him too often. Now she understood what the other nurses were talking about, why they gazed at him like lost puppies whenever he passed by.

"I appreciate your tact, Dr. Warmington."

She said it briskly and, her face still warmer than she'd like, she beat a hasty retreat before her own hormones went from simply gadding happily about in her system to having an actual full-on dance party.

He was too sexy for his own good—and hers.

Still smiling, David swiped a hand through his hair as the door closed behind Nychelle Cory. If anyone had told him he would smile after attending to a patient who might be losing her first child to miscarriage—especially one who seemed determined to blame her husband if it happened—he'd have said they were demented. It cut too close to home, brought the pain and regret that still haunted him after all these years into sharp focus.

If he closed his eyes he knew he'd instantly be able to bring Kitty's face to mind, see the anger and near hatred glittering in her eyes, hear the blame she'd spewed at him before walking out of their home and his life.

That wasn't something he dwelled on often; he knew she'd been devastated by the loss of their child, had lashed out at him as the only available target. But to have a patient come in at this time of the year, when the memories were so close to the surface anyway… Usually he'd be hard-pressed not to be overwhelmed by them, but now, instead, he clung to Nychelle's warmth and kept smiling.

Just seeing the nurse practitioner buzzing around the

clinic, dispensing that wide, sunny grin like instant relief medication, always gave him pleasure. This was one of the few times they'd interacted directly, but that was his own fault. When they'd first met, looking into those dark, gleaming eyes, seeing her gorgeous smile, had sent a sensation like an electric shock through his body, and he'd known immediately she was a woman to stay away from.

Agonizing memories were overshadowed by more enjoyable ones, and he closed his eyes, pictured Nychelle as he'd first seen her. Her hair had been pulled back into a simple bun, which had only emphasized the beauty of her oval face, her wide-set eyes and sweet, full mouth. Her smooth dark skin had been set off to perfection by a silky sunshine-yellow top that had done nothing to camouflage the high, rounded breasts beneath it, and her smart linen pants had showcased the rest of her glorious curves.

As far as he'd come from his rural roots, and as many lovely women as he'd met, something about Nychelle Cory had regressed him to the stuttering idiot he'd been in junior high school. She was intelligent and beautiful: the kind of woman men fantasized about finding and cherishing forever.

Making a family with.

But going down that road again wasn't an option he wanted even to contemplate. Having children was a dream that had died for him, and he didn't dare reawaken it. So, even if he was feeling that instinctive pull toward her, the smartest thing to do was to stay far away.

Painful memories threatened once more, the agony almost as sharp as it had been all those years ago. With a curse, David pulled his thoughts back from that precipice and reached for the tablet on his desk. He had notes to finish and an appointment due to begin any moment.

Yet his eyes strayed one more time to the door, and he remembered seeing Nychelle wiping away a tear as he came into the office. Apparently he wasn't the only one affected by their shared patient, and the knowledge of her tender-heartedness tugged at something deep in his chest.

Cursing again, he turned his attention to the digital device in his hand, determinedly putting all thoughts of the delectable nurse practitioner out of his head.

CHAPTER TWO

"This country has been so good to me, and it is my pleasure to be able to give back in some small way."

Crowded around the raised stage at the front of the school auditorium, the assembled doctors, nurse practitioners, RNs, medical and nursing students listened respectfully to Dr. Hamatty's pep talk.

It was a great turn-out, and Nychelle was cautiously confident that they were fully prepared for the influx of children who, brought by their parents, would soon be streaming in for the pediatric clinic. It had taken months of intense work by all the committee members to pull it together, but with Dr. Hamatty's connections they had assembled all the equipment and personnel they needed.

She'd been on site the evening before, helping to supervise the setting up of field hospital cubicles and examination tables, and directing the placement of diagnostic machines and dispensary. The Lauderlakes free clinics were famous for their quality of care—a point of pride for Dr. Hamatty, his staff and associates. Even the older, more established doctors turned out to lend their talents when time permitted.

In the middle of the group, Nychelle split her attention between the familiar speech and the conversation scrolling across her phone.

How much longer before you know for sure?

Aliya had added an excited face emoji for emphasis, making Nychelle smile. Anyone meeting her cousin in her guise as a rising young oncology researcher would never guess the depth of Aliya's silly side.

Already told you, another week and a half. Asking every day isn't going to speed up the process!

Are you going to cheat?

Nychelle smiled, shaking her head at how well her cousin knew her. The thought of buying one of those early detection pregnancy tests and taking it a couple of days before her next appointment *had* crossed her mind.

No. It would be like tempting fate.

A quick check found that Dr. Hamatty was at the point where he spoke about coming to the States as a child. His family had been poor, unable to speak proper English, and suffering the effects of the war-torn situation they'd left behind. After telling the story of how he'd got to where he was, he'd wrap it up and they'd all take their places, ready for the deluge of patients. He'd be another five, maybe seven minutes, she estimated.

Just enough time to finish her conversation with Aliya.

Without more than a glance at her phone, she typed her message.

Have you told your mom you won't be at the gala?

Yes. She's not amused, but agreed work had to come first.

Pursing her lips, Nychelle replied.

Not surprising at all.

To Dr. Monique Girvan work always came first. There had been a time when Nychelle had resented her mother for rarely being around, for putting her career advancement before everything else, up to and including her children. Now, although it still rankled, she'd learned to accept her mother for who she was.

It didn't mean her daughter had to walk in her footsteps, though. In fact, if anything, it made Nychelle determined not to. *Her* children wouldn't want for love, affection, and understanding.

Dr. Hamatty was getting close to winding up his speech, so Nychelle typed, Okay, almost go time. TTYL, then stuffed her phone into the pocket of her lab coat.

The crowd shifted, and muffled apologies following their movement as people bumped into one another. The nurse standing just in front of Nychelle turned to frown at the source of the disturbance, but her disapproving expression immediately faded and she lifted a hand to smooth her hair.

Following the other woman's gaze, Nychelle found herself face to face with David Warmington.

As usual his expression was serious, but there was a glint of a smile in his eyes and Nychelle was suddenly breathless, her heart stumbling as she drowned in the bright blue gaze.

He inched a little closer, surrounding her with the clean, fresh scent of utter maleness and, her legs suddenly wobbly, she turned back toward the stage, feigning the greatest of interest in the wrap-up of Dr. Hamatty's speech.

Keeping her head steadfastly trained forward, she contemplated with some annoyance the fact that the darn man was suddenly everywhere she looked. Over the last week it had felt as though she couldn't go two steps without seeing him. Worse, she'd found herself paying him far more attention than was warranted.

She had to admit, though, that what she'd seen was surprising, considering her previous assessment of his character. What she'd thought of as smooth charm seemed instead to be simply politeness. He never crossed the line into familiarity, and even seemed to display, on occasion, a touch of shyness.

He was unfailingly courteous, had a sly sense of humor, and he spoke to everyone from the janitorial staff to the senior partners in exactly the same way. Professionally, everyone agreed he was an excellent diagnostician and a thorough, diligent doctor.

Anyone hearing the nurses talk would believe him to be a paragon of every virtue, and Nychelle was beginning to understand why. He knew all their names, and she'd even overheard him asking one of the nurse aides about her son, who'd been ill the week before.

Once you got past his amazing looks, David Warmington seemed to be just a thoroughly nice person—but she knew better than to trust her own assessment of a man's character. She'd thought the same of Nick, and had been horribly wrong. She just wished she could get her hormones to remember how painful disappointment was, especially when it left you feeling used, so that they'd stop reacting to the man standing at her side.

"And now it's just about time to open the door and let our patients in." Dr. Hamatty beamed as he rubbed his hands together in what looked like anticipation. "Have a great, productive day, and on behalf of everyone involved in planning this I once more thank you for giving up your Saturday to help those in need."

There was a short round of applause as Dr. H. stepped

away from the microphone and the clinic committee chairperson stepped forward.

"Any latecomers who haven't received their instruction packages, please report to the intake table. Everyone else—please go to your assigned cubicle." She glanced at her watch. "We have fifteen minutes, folks."

Her smile was slightly strained, and Nychelle felt a pang of sympathy. It was no wonder almost every free clinic had a different coordinator. The stress of getting it all arranged was immense.

Clapping her hands together, like a schoolteacher trying to rally her students, and injecting a strident enthusiasm into her voice, the chairperson concluded, "Let's do this!"

As the crowd dispersed, Nychelle hesitated. She should acknowledge Dr. Warmington in some way, but was reluctant. Ridiculous as it might be, just thinking of meeting his intent gaze made goose bumps fire down her spine and had her nipples tightening to tingling peaks.

"This is quite some set-up. I wasn't sure what to expect."

His words were obviously directed at her, since she was the only one left standing in the immediate vicinity.

Silently admonishing herself to stay cool, Nychelle made the half turn necessary to face him. Thankfully he was taking in the room, his gaze on the dispensary across the gymnasium.

Before she could answer, he continued, "I don't think I've ever seen a pharmacy at a free clinic."

Okay, this was a safe topic to talk about, and since she wasn't skewered by that intense gaze Nychelle relaxed.

"Dr. Hamatty had to work really hard to get a special license for it. Apparently he realized, after the first few clinics he arranged, that it didn't help the patients if they were given prescriptions they couldn't afford to fill. All the medications are donated and, with a few exceptions, they're limited to mostly over-the-counter drugs, so eventually he was allowed to have it."

Nychelle couldn't help chuckling softly, before continuing, "Dr. H. has a lot of clout in the medical community, and beyond. It was inconceivable they'd be able to hold out against him forever."

As though drawn by the sound of her laughter, David looked at her, and immediately she was snared. Really, was it fair for a man to have eyes like that? So gorgeous they made a girl's heart stop for a second and then had it galloping like an out-of-control horse?

No, Nychelle decided. No, it wasn't in the slightest bit fair.

David's lips quirked at the corners and amusement lit his eyes again. "Somehow I'm not surprised. Dr. H. is a powerhouse. I doubt anyone says no to him. Not more than once anyway." He waved his hand in an abbreviated arc, gesturing to the room at large. "The number of us here is testimony to that."

Had he *wanted* to say no? Wasn't being charitable a part of his nature?

Unaccountably disappointed at the thought, she asked, "You weren't at the last one? I would have thought you'd be roped in from the start."

David briefly lifted one shoulder in what she'd come to realize was a characteristic shrug. "I had already committed to going to Los Angeles to finish a course on genetic counseling for oncology patients. Dr. H. knew about it when he hired me, so knew I wouldn't be at the free clinic. I assured him I'd happily participate going forward."

He looked down at the information package in his hand. "I should try to find my spot." Glancing up at the alphabetically arranged banners hanging from the ceiling, he continued, "I'm in D section, cubicle five."

"I'm just two cubicles down from you, so I can show you where it is."

"Oh, good."

He gave her a full, beaming smile, and the breath seized in her throat.

"So I can run to you if I have any questions?"

"Um…" Nychelle swallowed to make sure her voice wasn't breathy and ridiculous before she attempted to answer. "Somehow I doubt you'll need my help. I, on the other hand, am glad to know I'm in close proximity to the polyglot doctor."

Wanting to lighten her emotional response to his smile, she narrowed her eyes, giving him a mock glare.

"You *do* speak several languages, right? You weren't just pulling my leg?"

With a touch on her arm, which even through her lab coat caused a burst of heat over her skin, David guided her around to face their section and began to walk. Nychelle fell in beside him, keeping her attention on where she was going rather than looking up at the stunning profile of the man beside her.

"Spanish and Portuguese, French, Italian and some German—enough to get by anyway. A little Arabic and a smattering of Hindi. I can understand a bit of Mandarin, but just the basics. I've been told my Cantonese is a disgrace, but once the person I'm talking to stops laughing I can carry on a conversation…"

That last bit was said in such a disgruntled tone Nychelle couldn't help giggling. "Okay, okay—I believe you."

"Oh." David paused abruptly, just before they got to their assigned areas. "I actually sought you out to let you know that Mrs. Cardozo and her baby are in no danger, and she's been cleared by Dr. Tza to fly back home next week."

Nychelle was about to ask for more details when the

coordinator's voice boomed through the auditorium. "Ten minutes, people. Ten minutes."

"Oops, better get going." Nychelle smiled up at David, was rewarded by an answering grin. Then she asked, "Did Dr. Tza's office call with the update?"

"No, I called to follow up. See you."

He strode toward his assigned examination area and warmth flooded Nychelle's chest. Checking on a patient he'd only seen once and likely wouldn't see again was beyond his purview, but knowing he'd done so made her unreasonably happy.

Get a grip on yourself. You're getting as bad as the other nurses!

But the admonishment couldn't wipe away the smile on her lips.

"I'm going to suggest going back to your old detergent. The location of the rash seems to indicate contact dermatitis, and the recent change to a different brand of laundry soap seems the obvious culprit."

As the elderly man and preteen boy David was escorting out paused at the entrance to the examination area David continued. "The hydrocortisone cream will help with the itching, but if you go back to the old detergent and the rash doesn't clear up in about a month, you'll need to have him examined again."

The old man nodded, then held out a gnarled and wrinkled hand to shake.

"Thanks, Doctor." He shook his head and grumbled, "Darn kids. That new brand is cheaper than the old one. Wouldn't you know one of them would be allergic?"

But, despite his grousing, he slung his arm around the boy's shoulders as they walked away, and the youngster looped his own arm around the waist of the man he'd called

"Grandpa." Clearly there was genuine affection between the pair.

It was funny, David mused, how freely people talked about their lives in the short period of time they had with him in this clinic setting. Already today he'd heard myriad stories about difficult circumstances—like Mr. Jones and Tyrell, the pair now making their way to the dispensary. Mr. Jones wasn't even the boy's blood relative, but was married to Tyrell's great-aunt, who'd taken Tyrell and his two sisters in after their mother went to jail. A sad story in a way, and yet a testament to people's innate goodness.

David could relate to many of the stories of poverty. After all, he'd lived it, and it really wasn't that long since he'd broken away from the grinding cycle of just trying to survive.

Sometimes it felt as if it were yesterday he'd been patching his shoes with newspaper and wearing clothes donated to the family by charitable organizations. Often he caught himself reverting to type—hesitating to buy something he could definitely afford because the price was still shocking to him on an almost visceral level, or rinsing a jar to save instead of putting it into the recycling. Some habits were definitely harder to break than others when they'd been acquired at a really young age.

About to call for the next patient in line, he glanced toward where Nychelle was working, just in time to see her trying to get his attention. He stayed where he was for a moment, allowing himself to enjoy the sight of her hurrying toward him. Even in a pair of pink scrubs printed with pictures of bunnies and teddy bears under a generic white lab coat, her face bare of makeup except for a slick of lip gloss, Nychelle was beautiful.

The only thing missing was her habitual smile. Instead her mouth was set in a firm line, and noticing that had him moving to meet her in front of the examination area that separated their assigned areas.

"Dr. Warmington, if you're free I'd appreciate your assistance."

Her voice was level, without inflection, but David searched her eyes, saw the hint of deep emotion she was trying hard to subdue.

"Of course. What's the problem?"

"I have a toddler—male, three years old, underweight—with jaundice and an elevated temperature, and a Haitian mother who doesn't speak much English, so I can't get an accurate history."

She turned to lead the way to her area.

"What are you thinking?"

Nychelle sent him a worried glance over her shoulder. "I don't know how long they've been in the country, so until I do I can't rule out malaria or Hep A—although it would be unusual for a toddler to show symptoms of hepatitis."

Children that young, he knew, were usually asymptomatic when they contracted Hep A, and quickly recovered without treatment. The real danger would be the chance of the child passing Hepatitis A on to others around him, especially if they were living in less than hygienic conditions.

"Without a history I can't rule out sickle cell anemia or Gilbert's syndrome either."

She paused outside the curtain surrounding her examination area, and David could hear the little boy fussing and the sounds of his mother hushing him without success.

Nychelle shook her head, her frustration patently clear for an instant. "I'm pretty much dead in the water without knowing more." Then she squeezed his wrist—just a quick, strong clasp of her long fingers—and said, "I'm so glad I have you to call on."

Then she slipped between the curtains, leaving him there

trying to catch his breath and get a grip on his suddenly wayward libido.

Who knew that one little touch could be as effective as a striptease?

Cursing himself, he ruthlessly pushed away all imaginings of what it would be like to have Nychelle Cory's fingers on other parts of his body, and then followed her through the curtain.

The mother looked harried, and instinctively David held out his arms to the little boy. Big brown eyes widening, the toddler stopped crying and gave David a considering look. Then, after a hiccup, he smiled and tipped forward right into David's grasp.

As he caught the little boy, and then settled the slight weight against his chest, David took a quick inventory. The little fellow was definitely warm, and the sclera of both eyes had a distinctive yellow tint. Time to figure out what was going on.

So, putting on his most calming smile, he turned to the little boy's mother. *"Bonjour, madame. Puis-je vous poser quelques questions?"*

CHAPTER THREE

NYCHELLE SIGHED AS she stepped into the kitchen of her South Fort Lauderdale bungalow and pulled the door closed. Putting down her tote bag, she toed off her shoes, appreciating the cool air indoors, so different from the heat of her garage. Twisting her head first one way and then the other, she tried to work out the tension tightening her neck muscles.

Although each of the medical personnel were only asked to work a three-hour shift at the free clinic, she knew extra hands were always needed at the patient intake booth, or as troubleshooters for the other medical practitioners, and she'd offered her services.

The afternoon had flown by, and before she'd even realized it the clinic had been winding down, so she'd stayed until it ended at five. She was tired—maybe even more so than she'd usually be—but as she yawned widely a feeling of accomplishment made the weariness bearable.

Barefoot, she wandered into the kitchen to retrieve a bottle of water from her fridge, grabbing a handful of grapes at the same time.

The day had been a resounding success, as usual, yet a nagging sense of discontent dogged her every move, and she wasn't able to put her finger on the source. Stifling another yawn behind the water bottle in her hand, she considered having a nice soak and an evening of watching some of the myriad TV shows she'd recorded.

Usually there would be some wine thrown into the mix for good measure but, of course, that wasn't in the cards right now. Hopefully wouldn't be for another thirty-nine weeks.

There was no stopping the grin stretching her lips to the maximum, nor the little thrill trickling down her spine. No matter what else was bothering her, the prospect of a baby—*her* baby—made it all okay.

She was still smiling as she put the grapes in a bowl and then headed across the living room toward her bedroom to prepare her bath.

When her cell phone rang, the distinctive sound of Beethoven's *Fifth* made her good humor all but evaporate. A little groan escaped before she could stop it, and the immediate wave of guilt that brought had her shaking her head.

Reversing course, she strode back toward the kitchen, hurrying so as not to miss the call. Dumping the water bottle and bowl on the console table, she launched a frantic rummage in her bag to find her phone. Locating it under her wadded-up lab coat, she swiped the screen and brought it up to her ear.

"Hi, Mom."

"Nychelle. How did the clinic go?"

Not *How are you?* or *What are you up to?* Nope—straight to work. Sometimes Nychelle wondered if that was all herself and her mother had in common. The thought irritated her more than usual tonight, and she had to temper her annoyance so it wouldn't show in her voice.

"It went very well. We had approximately two thousand patients come through."

"When will you be taking on the chairperson position? Haven't you been asked?"

Nychelle took a deep breath, willing herself not to react to the obvious implication of her mother's last question.

"I was asked, but I didn't accept."

Before her mother could launch into another lecture about ambition and the necessity of taking on hard tasks so as to be able to advance in the workplace, Nychelle continued.

"I was in the middle of those skill improvement courses Dr. Hamatty requested we all take. To be honest, I wanted to make sure I didn't just complete them, but aced them."

"Hmph."

Nychelle knew her mother still wanted to take her to task for not accepting the position anyway, but really couldn't, since her reason for not doing so was also work-related.

"Well, I suggest taking it on if it's offered to you again. But don't be surprised if it isn't. Many of the best opportunities come along only once. Rarely are there second chances in life."

Nychelle bit her lip, holding back a snort of laughter. Her mother would have a fit if she knew Nychelle had already gotten another chance to chair the committee and had once again asked to defer to one of the other committee members.

"Also, I want you to make sure you're on time for the pre-gala reception next Saturday."

Having said her piece on one subject, her mother had swiftly moved on to the next. She probably had a list of points to touch on written out in front of her.

"I know it's embarrassing to come to these functions by yourself, but please endeavor to arrive early. If you lived closer to Martin, he and Jennifer could pick you up, but your house is too out of the way to be convenient."

Another one of her mother's thinly veiled criticisms. While her parents and her cousin Martin all lived in the northern end of the city, in far more expensive neighborhoods, Nychelle had chosen to live in the trendier and more affordable South Fort Lauderdale. It was a nice area, but the way her parents talked about it anyone would be forgiven for thinking it a slum.

"No problem, Mom. The hotel isn't that far from here, so it wouldn't make sense to have someone pick me up anyway. And, yes, I'll be there early enough for the reception."

"Do you have something appropriate to wear?"

Nychelle allowed the chuckle she'd been holding in to escape.

"Not yet, Mom." Her mother didn't wear the same formal dress twice, and expected the same from her daughters. "I plan to go and buy something this week."

She actually didn't plan to buy a new dress. For her, the outfit she'd worn to a friend's wedding would be suitable—but she wouldn't be telling her mother that. No. She'd avoid the lecture until later, then just say she'd been too busy with work to get something.

"Leaving it a little late, aren't you?"

Shaking her head, Nychelle picked up the water bottle from where she'd put it on the console table and, juggling it, her phone and the bowl of grapes, started back across the living room.

Suddenly exhausted, all she wanted was that longed-for bath and a chance to relax: impossible to do with her mother on the other end of the phone.

"I haven't had a chance before. You know how it is. Work must come first."

Unfair, perhaps, to quote her mother's words back at her, but it should be an effective topic-closer.

Yet it wasn't.

"The annual Medical Association charity gala is where you'll find all the movers and shakers of the Florida medical community assembled in one place. You need to make a good impression."

"Yes, Mom. I know." If there was one thing her parents had drummed into their daughters, it was that connections were important when it came to building a career. "One day I might be applying to one of them for a job."

If she'd had more energy she'd have pointed out that Dr. Hamatty, arguably one of the most influential doctors in the city, had hired her without knowing anything about her other than her credentials. Tonight she just felt as if she'd be battering her head against a wall.

"Exactly. Well, I'll let you go. See you next Saturday."

And just like that, without waiting for Nychelle to reply, her mother hung up.

"Wow, Mom. Bye to you too," she said to the dial tone, before throwing her phone onto the bed.

While she undressed, she carried on the imaginary conversation. "And how's Dad? Oh, I'm glad to hear his shoulder is better. How was the surgical conference? Will his latest paper be published?"

Still grumbling to herself, she filled the bathtub and added a sprinkle of bath salts, hoping to soak out the aches of the long, busy day. Sinking into the warm water, she released a long sigh and willed herself to relax.

There was no changing her parents at this late stage, so it didn't make sense to let their attitude toward her life and her career stress her out. Especially now. When she told them she was pregnant there'd be no excitement or joy, just more disapproval, so best she prepare for it.

Realizing she was grinding her teeth, she sank a little deeper into the tub and, forcibly dismissing old hurts, turned her thoughts to the day just past.

Immediately David Warmington came to mind, and she smiled as she remembered little Etienne, the Haitian toddler, throwing himself out of his mother's arms into David's. Children of that age were notorious for clinging to their parents, especially if they weren't feeling well, but

Etienne had hardly hesitated before happily going to the doctor.

Not that Nychelle blamed the little boy in the slightest. She'd found herself wanting to throw herself into Dr. Warmington's arms too. Which was ridiculous—and no doubt caused by some strange chemical reaction that all the IUI drugs had created in her brain. Yes, he was gorgeous, seemed nice, and was sexy as hell—but those weren't good excuses to be panting after him. In fact they were all great reasons to avoid him like the plague.

Besides, even if she had been tempted, now she knew for sure David Warmington would never be the man for her even if the circumstances had been different.

Suddenly wanting to move, to be active, even though the whole point of the bath was to relax, she sat up and reached for her body wash, shivering slightly as the cooler air touched her shoulders and breasts when they rose out of the water.

It wasn't a conversation she should even have been privy to, but it wasn't as though she'd eavesdropped on purpose. She'd just happened to be sitting at the table behind David and Dr. Tomkins, one of the other doctors from Lauderlakes, in the cafeteria during her lunch break. Besides, neither had made any effort to keep their voice down, so they obviously hadn't had any expectation of privacy. Mind you, Dr. Tomkins had a voice like a cannon, his words booming out in ear-shocking volleys.

"Dr. H. mentioned to me that the parents are very impressed by you, David. Saying how well you handle their kids. Maybe you should have gone into pediatrics."

When David had replied he'd sounded neither gratified nor amused. "No...no pediatrics for me. It was never an option."

Dr. Tomkins had chuckled. "Well, at least when you

have children of your own you should have a good rapport with them, if today was any indication."

"That's something else I don't consider an option."

Had it been her imagination, or had his voice been cold—not like his usual mellow tones? Without being able to see his face she hadn't been sure, but the alacrity with which Dr. Tomkins had changed the subject had Nychelle suspecting she was right.

Shaking her head, she sank back into the water and frowned. Another man who professed not to want kids—probably for some damned selfish reason too. Nick had said he'd consider children once his career was more settled, although he was already well on his way. Now Nychelle couldn't help wondering what David's reason was. He didn't strike her as the selfish type.

Charm, which Nick had exhibited in abundance, was something she'd learned could be easily feigned, and it differed markedly from good character and genuine caring. Even her father, normally coolly distant, had the ability to turn on the charm when he thought it worthwhile.

Nychelle couldn't help wondering if the real David was hiding behind a thin veneer of charisma, like the one Nick had. Not that it mattered to her. She couldn't care less. Wouldn't allow herself to care.

What truly irked her, though, was her physical reaction to David, since she should know better than to be attracted to another charmer.

As she lay back in the water, it wasn't the popping of the soap bubbles floating away from her skin that raised goose bumps on her arms and chest and made her nipples tighten and tingle. It was the memory of watching David's hands as he'd worked, hearing the warm cadence of his voice as he'd soothed the patient and his mother, and the breathlessness she'd felt each time his gaze caught hers or she looked at his lips.

With a little groan of surrender Nychelle swept a palm over one breast, succumbing to the lure of a fantasy in which David Warmington pulled her close to his strong body and kissed her until she turned to putty in those gorgeous hands.

And somehow she knew those hands, lips and body could bring her more pleasure than she'd ever known before.

"Cut it out, Nychelle."

Saying it out loud didn't stop the ache building in her core, and with a growl of frustration she slapped both palms down on the surface of the water, inadvertently splashing herself in the face.

"Oh, for crying out loud!"

Spluttering, she wiped the soapy water from her cheeks, then laughed as she reached for a towel to dry her eyes. It was the kind of silly thing she'd usually share with Aliya, but in this case probably wouldn't. The last thing she needed was to get in the habit of talking to her cousin about David. Aliya would definitely pick up on hearing his name over and over again.

Despite claiming to understand why Nychelle was undergoing IUI, her cousin had tried to convince her to wait a little longer before having a baby.

"There's a man out there for you," Aliya had said over lunch the last time she'd come to Florida for a visit. "I know Nick broke your heart, and you're probably not ready to trust yet, but give it a little more time."

Just the sound of her ex-fiancé's name had made a sour taste rise into the back of her throat, and Nychelle had shaken her head. "It's not about Nick."

When Aliya's eyebrows had gone up, Nychelle had known her cousin didn't believe her.

"It's not *all* about Nick," she'd qualified. "Yes, he broke my heart, but that was a couple of years ago, and I'm over it."

"Are you really?" Aliya had pressed the point. "You were with him for years, and he used our family connections to advance his career. Then he cheated on you and got some other girl pregnant after telling you he wasn't ready to have a child yet. I'd have a hard time getting over that. And the fact you won't even consider waiting to find someone else tells me you're anything but over it."

"I don't need a relationship to get what I want." She raised her hand to stop her cousin launching into a rebuttal. "And I don't have time to build one, to learn to trust again, before I start trying to conceive."

"But..."

"No. You know that with the scarring on my uterus the longer I wait to try to start a family the harder it will be. Realistically, I'm almost thirty, and at the optimal time in my life—physically, financially and emotionally—to start a family. I don't want to wait, hoping I'll meet someone, and miss this chance."

Aliya's expression had softened, and she'd said, "From when you were little you said you wanted a big family. I guess that's never changed."

"Exactly. So I'm going to do the IUI and let the rest of it take care of itself." Then she'd added, just so Aliya wouldn't figure out she wasn't planning even to consider another relationship and get on her case, "If there's someone out there for me he'll find me, or I'll find him. If not, it's not a big deal."

"Huh." Disgruntlement had radiated from Aliya's snort. "I still think waiting a couple years more wouldn't hurt."

Now, as Nychelle stepped out of the tub, she reached down to touch her belly, skimming her fingertips over the place where, hopefully, her baby was growing and thriving. “It’s okay that it’s just you and me, sweetie. We really don’t need anyone else.”

Funny how suddenly the words had a bittersweet quality—but she didn’t want to consider why that might be. Instead, she gave her reflection a bracing nod, then turned away to reach for her towel. This was the best time of her life and nothing would make her regret trying for a baby.

Nothing.

CHAPTER FOUR

THERE WAS SOMETHING a little off about David Warmington today, but Nychelle couldn't put her finger on it. Perhaps it was that for the first time she sensed he was growing ever more irritated with a patient.

Not that she could blame him. Douglas Comstock, a sports agent referred to the clinic by one of his star clients, was being willfully difficult. He'd come in complaining of persistent leg pain, and after examining him she'd sent him for X-rays and a MRI. He had requested pain medication, because over-the-counter painkillers were no longer working, and since nurse practitioners weren't allowed to prescribe medication Nychelle had requested one of the GPs see him. David had been available.

Now she was being treated to a battle of wills, her head swiveling back and forth between the two men as though she were at a debate. It would be entertaining if it weren't for the fact she was sure David was having a hard time dealing with this patient.

As she watched, it seemed David took a deeper than necessary breath before saying, "Mr. Comstock—"

"Doug." The man grinned, totally at ease. Almost seeming to be enjoying himself. "Call me Doug, Doc."

"Doug. I'm going to refer you to Dr. Napoli, who is one of the best orthopedic surgeons in Florida. But, I'm telling you, she's not going to be able to help you until you lose some weight."

Doug Comstock was still smiling, even as he shook his head. "Don't bother sending me to anyone else. Just give me some meds, Doc, and I'll be on my way. As I was telling Nychelle, that losing weight thing's probably just not going to happen. I'm on the road for most of the year, traveling with the athletes I manage, and I don't have time to add anything else to my schedule, you know?"

He made the argument sound reasonable, but David was having none of it.

"No," he countered. "I don't know. Explain to me how eating healthier and getting exercise are going to disrupt your schedule."

"Sure, Doc."

Doug kept right on smiling, and Nychelle realized it was probably part of the reason he was successful. It was an effective way to rebuff almost any dissent.

"I'm at sporting events most nights, or out scouting new talent. Then there are after-parties or press conferences. Even if there are no events there are dinners, where I'm schmoozing prospective clients or dealing with owners. I'm up with the birds, on the phone making connections, setting things up, talking to people on the other side of the world. Then I'm taking people to lunch, or sitting around in meetings most of the day. My day is long, and as full as you can get, and it involves a lot of eating and drinking to boot. Add one more thing into that and I have to drop something else. What do you suggest? The three or four hours of sleep I get a night?"

While his pleasant expression hadn't changed, there was a steely tone in his voice. He obviously wasn't used to being lectured or opposed, but once more David didn't back down.

"I see from the chart Nurse Cory tried to schedule you for some tests, but you told her not to set them up."

"Yup." Doug shifted on the table, lifting one beefy leg and then the other, obviously uncomfortable although his smile remained in place. "I'm heading to Taiwan in three days, so it doesn't make sense for her to bother. I won't make the appointments anyway."

David glanced at Nychelle and she gave him a quick upward quirk of her eyebrows. A silent *good luck*. Then David gave Doug a thoughtful look. Normally by now he should be telling the patient to put on his clothes and come into the adjacent office, where they could sit and discuss the situation in comfort. Instead, perhaps to underscore the importance of what he had to say, David launched right in.

"Okay, Mr. Comstock. I know I should probably be more tactful, but I don't think you'll take me seriously. So I'm going to give this to you straight."

Was that a slight wavering of the smile on their patient's face? Nychelle couldn't be sure, but she hoped so. It might mean the other man was really listening.

"You're at least a hundred pounds over the optimal weight for your height and bone structure. I suspect, from the X-rays and MRI results, that you may have a herniated disc, which accounts for the leg pain, and the numbness and weakness you're experiencing. While there are treatments that could help with the pain, those are best explored with a specialist like Dr. Napoli. Realistically, though, the treatment is probably going to be ineffective if you don't address the root causes of the problem. And pain medication on its own will only mask the symptoms."

"But—"

David gave the man a stern look and held up one hand. "Wait, please. Let me finish."

Smile totally gone, Doug gave a little huff of clear annoyance, but subsided.

"Perhaps even more important, even at your age, your weight puts you at risk for so many other diseases. Ones that can halt you right in your busy tracks."

He glanced down at the tablet in his hand, maybe to give his words a chance to sink in, then continued.

"Your blood pressure is elevated, and although you're on the appropriate medication you say you haven't been to a doctor in a few years, so I suspect your management of that hasn't been tracked, nor your medication adjusted. Uncontrolled blood pressure can lead to a stroke."

Doug's eyes widened slightly, but David pressed on, relentless in a way she suspected he normally wouldn't be. Seeing him like this was a little surreal.

And surprisingly attractive.

She shook that thought away, but not before a little tingle had tiptoed down her spine.

"You're also at an elevated risk for diabetes—which, should you develop it, would definitely add new tasks to your daily routine, such as taking your blood sugar levels three times a day and giving yourself injections of insulin to ensure you don't go into a diabetic coma."

Doug Comstock paled. His lips parted, but then he looked down and closed them again. David waited and then, assured the other man wouldn't interrupt, he continued.

"Nurse Cory has noted you've had some breathing issues, which could be something as simple as a reaction to air quality or as serious as imminent congestive heart failure. I'm also concerned about your cholesterol levels, considering your lifestyle, but there is no way to know whether you should be worried about either of those matters without further tests. Furthermore, your excess weight, as well as putting undue pressure on your back, is also putting immense pressure on your other joints, so you can expect to begin experiencing knee, hip and/or ankle problems. Also, with all the traveling you do, you are definitely at risk for deep vein thrombosis. Do you know what that is?"

A now somber Doug shook his head. David definitely had his attention now, thank goodness.

"That is when blood clots form in your legs, which can then travel through the veins and cause a pulmonary embolism—a blockage in your lungs. You have two of the major risk factors—you sit down a lot, and you're overweight."

Sensing the patient's rising anxiety, Nychelle stepped closer, and said, "Mr. Comstock, I know it seems like a real inconvenience to try to lose weight, or to concentrate on your health when you have so much going on, and so many people depending on you, but we can help. Make it achievable without adding too much fuss to your day."

She smiled, hoping to soften the words. It was like playing "good cop, bad cop," and if it would help to get the patient on the right track, she was willing to go with it.

"I..." Doug Comstock frowned, then looked down again at his hands, where they lay on his thighs. "I guess I can at least try. I haven't been feeling so good lately, and I'm not sleeping well, but I just put it down to the pain."

David opened his mouth, and Nychelle hoped he wouldn't bring up any of the other myriad conditions obesity might be causing the patient, like sleep apnea. There was no point in overloading Doug with *what ifs* and risk him shutting down. Not now, when he seemed amenable to letting them guide him to a healthier way of life.

But instead David said, "Why don't you put on your clothes and come through to the office? We'll get you scheduled for some blood tests—many of which we can do right now, before you leave—and Nurse Cory and I will set you up with a plan to get you on the right track."

"Okay. Okay." Doug heaved himself off the table. "I've only gotten this big in the last six years, since my management business took off, believe it or not."

"That's actually good," David said. "It's not the habits of a lifetime you're trying to break, just those you've developed over a short space of time. I think, for a man of your drive and character, this will be a breeze."

And Doug, thankfully, was smiling again as David and Nychelle left the room.

David was hard pressed to remember when last he'd been so annoyed with a patient and, given the thoughtful look Nychelle sent him as they entered her office, he guessed he hadn't hidden it very well.

"Whew," Nychelle said quietly, after making sure the door to the examination room was firmly closed. David was already on the defensive, even before she said, "I'm glad you got through to Mr. Comstock, but you were pretty hard on him."

"He needed me to be."

He realized how much of a growl that had been when Nychelle glanced at him again, her eyebrows raised.

But all she said was, "Apparently. I said a lot of the same things to him and all he did was brush me off. I was a little worried he was prescription shopping, when he kept insisting all he needed were painkillers."

As she crossed to the credenza where she kept various informational brochures, David went to sit at her desk and blew out a long breath.

"At least we cleared up that misapprehension, but I honestly have no idea whether he'll actually listen to us and try to make the changes we suggest." He pulled the laptop closer to bring up the necessary records. "Sometimes I wonder why we bother."

Pausing in the midst of pulling pamphlets from a drawer, Nychelle sent him a steady look over her shoulder. "It can frustrating at times, I know." Turning back to her chore, she asked, quietly, "Everything okay?"

"Yes." Yet, he could hear the lie in his voice—feel it in the jagged ache that fired through his chest. "I'm fine."

Thankfully she didn't reply immediately, allowing him to continue selecting the tests he wanted the patient to undergo on the electronic form. It was easier to concentrate on that than to think about what today meant, or let Nychelle's instinctive kindness undo all the emotional barriers he'd marshaled to get him through the day.

He didn't look up from the computer screen when she came across to the desk, not even when she said, "Well, if you need anything—an ear, or a hand—just let me know."

Her compassion was almost his undoing, and he was thankful when the door to the exam room opened and Douglas Comstock came in to join them.

After Nychelle had taken their rather subdued patient off to have some of the tests run, David made his way back to his own office. Dropping into his chair, he scrubbed both hands over his face, as though to awaken himself from the aching sorrow wrapped around him like a pall. He should have taken the day off, but the thought of being at home without anything to do had had zero appeal, and there was nowhere he could think of going that would have been any better. Work seemed the best way to deal with the pain.

How tempted he'd been to tell Nychelle what today was. Something in her empathetic gentle gaze, the timbre of her voice, had made him want to share with her that which he never shared. Had never been tempted to share, neither wanting to worsen the wound nor, conversely, diminish the loss. As if saying the words *Today was the day my baby girl, my Natalie, was born way too early and didn't survive* would be a betrayal of the love he still felt ten years later.

She had been born at just shy of twenty weeks. As a doctor he would call it a miscarriage or, worse, a spontaneous abortion. As a man, Natalie's father, he couldn't bring himself to think of it that way. It was simply her birthday, the day he'd truly learned, for the first time, what love was. And it was also the day he'd learned the immensity of the agony love could cause. The irrevocable, heartbreaking loss hadn't become easier to bear over time. Probably never would.

Taking a breath, he held it for a moment and then blew it out. Leaning back in his chair, he wished he were still in Chicago so he could visit her grave, the way he had every other year. When he'd been offered the job in Florida he'd thought about moving away from her and almost refused. Yet he'd known it was time to move on—not from her, but in his professional life. He'd reassured himself he didn't need to be there to remember her, to miss her, but he hadn't realized how bad today would be, the pain magnified by distance and the strangeness of his new life.

What he needed was something that would center him, pull him back from the dark clouds threatening to overtake his spirit. It was at times like this he wished he could call Kitty. As Natalie's mother, he knew she would share his grief, but Kitty had a new life, a husband who could comfort her, and two other children to think about. A few years after the divorce their contact had dwindled away to Christmas cards only—the last acknowledgment of what they'd shared and always would. His struggle to cope with this anniversary was no reason for him to encroach on her life and perhaps make it worse for her too.

No, he had to accept that nothing would take away his pain today, but there was one person who could at least dull it.

So he picked up the phone and dialed.

After a couple of rings, the receiver on the other end was picked up and his mother said, "Davie. I wondered if you'd call today."

Just hearing her voice eased the band of heartache around his chest. Leaning back in his office chair and rocking slightly back and forth, he listened to his mother's melodic voice coming through on speakerphone. He knew she wouldn't mention Natalie—that wasn't her way—but just hearing her voice as she spoke about the family and doings in the tiny town he was born in leeched more of the tension from his body.

His computer pinged, and he leaned forward to look at the message his receptionist had sent.

Nurse Cory is asking for a few moments of your time when you're finished on the phone.

Stress—different from what he'd felt before when thinking about Natalie, but just as potent—tightened his shoulders and neck. She probably wanted to bring him up to speed on Doug Comstock, and he was tempted to ask her to leave a note for him rather than have to see her again. Being around her unsettled something deep inside him, stirred feelings he didn't want to examine. Yet, he found himself typing…

Send her in, Trina.

CHAPTER FIVE

A FEW SECONDS later the door opened just far enough for Nychelle's face to appear in the crack between it and the jamb. When she hesitated, raising an eyebrow, he waved her in. She glanced at the phone before slipping into the room and closing the door behind her, and he suddenly realized she looked tired. There were little bags under her eyes which, in the midst of his own self-absorption, he hadn't noticed earlier and now wondered about.

He'd lost track of the conversation with his mother and now, not taking his gaze off Nychelle, tried to catch up with what Momma was saying.

"Then Ms. Lattimore refused to contribute to the bake sale, because she felt slighted, and I had to give her a firm talking-to." Momma gave a huff of annoyance. "Told her that's no way for a grown lady and a parishioner to behave. In the end she made a dozen of her pecan pies, after saying she'd never do a thing for the church again if Janie Carruthers was running the charity committee."

Nychelle's lips twitched, then spread into a smile as she settled into the chair across the desk from him. If it were anyone else David would have hesitated to allow them to be privy to his conversation, but for some reason he didn't mind Nychelle hearing his mother ramble on.

"You're a born peacemaker, Momma. Should have been a police officer."

"Go on with you."

Her laughter trickled through the office, and David smiled to hear it.

"You're so silly, Davie."

Nychelle covered her mouth with one hand, but not before a little burst of laughter escaped.

"Someone there with you, Davie?"

The gleam of laughter in Nychelle's eyes increased at hearing his nickname again, and David sent her a mock glare as he replied, "One of the nurse practitioners, Nurse Cory, just came in, Momma."

"Oh, you're busy. I should let you go."

"Wait, Momma." He'd almost forgotten to mention one of the reasons he'd called. "Have you and Poppa given any more thought about coming down for a visit? I have the spare room all ready for you."

He knew what she was going to say before she said it, just from the few moments of silence before she replied.

"You know what your poppa is like, Davie. Always working...never wanting to take a break. Besides—*Florida*?"

She said it as though it were outer space, rather than just a couple states away. Not that strange, since the farthest his parents had traveled before they'd reluctantly flown to Maryland for his graduation from medical school was to Charleston, about an hour away from their home. The reluctance in her voice was clear, when she said, "I don't know..."

"Well, think about it, okay? Now that Jessa is out of school I'm sure she and Little Bub could help Mary-Liz for a little while at the shop." He well knew his sister could probably manage their dad's business by herself, but her kids would probably be glad to earn some pocket money over the summer.

"I'll ask him, Davie."

Skepticism was rife in her voice, and he knew her agreeing to ask his father again was the best he could hope for.

"Now, I'll let you get back to work."

"Okay, Momma. Love—"

But, with a click, she was gone before he could finish. Shaking his head, David reached over to disconnect the speaker, cutting off the buzz of the dial tone.

"Ah. Your mom belongs to the Dr. Monique Girvan school of telephone conversations." Nychelle was still smiling, but the laughter had faded from her eyes. "As soon as she's finished talking she hangs up."

Leaning back, he asked, "Dr. Monique Girvan?" Why was that name so familiar?

"My mother."

"Ah..." He still wasn't sure where he'd heard the name before, but gave Nychelle a half smile. "I'd suggest it's a mom thing, but I think my mom was just a little flustered to think I was supposed to be working. What I do for a living is a bit of a mystery to her. Her experience of doctors is limited to what she's seen on TV and the old family practitioner in our little town, who's always rushing around, busier than a one-armed coat hanger."

"Busier than...?" Nychelle started to giggle. "Where did you get an expression like that?"

Her laughter was contagious and, inexplicably lighthearted, he chuckled before replying. "My roommate in college was from Canada, and he used that expression all the time. I like it."

He moved an invitation he'd left on his desk from side to side, wanting something to do with his hands. The sudden urge to put them on Nychelle Cory—trace the sweet, smooth lines of her cheeks and neck, rub his thumb across the soft pillow of her lower lip—was shocking, and he quickly squelched it.

"I can see why." She was still giggling a little. Then she added, *"Davie,"* in a credible facsimile of his mother's accent, and they both dissolved into full-blown laughter.

Strangely, he didn't feel the least abashed at her teasing, although he knew himself to be touchy about his poor, Low Country roots. Even stranger was how their shared laughter lightened the darkness still swirling in his soul, pushing it and his lingering grief back just a bit more.

"South Carolina?" she asked, after she could talk again. "I've been trying to figure your accent out, but it really only became pronounced when I heard you talking to your mom."

"I've moved around a lot in the last twelve years, and lost most of my accent. It seems to come back when I'm talking to my family."

"Mine does too. I've lived in the States since I was ten, but if you hear me on the phone with my cousin Aliya you'd think I just got off the plane from Jamaica."

She reached up to tuck an errant strand of hair back into her bun, causing her blouse to tighten across her breasts, and David forced his gaze away from the alluring sight. What on earth was wrong with him, ogling her every chance he got? Hopefully she hadn't noticed what he was doing.

As she straightened in her chair, her gaze fell to the invitation he was still shifting from hand to hand across the surface of his desk. "Is that an invitation to the FMA charity gala?"

Surprised by the change in the conversation, David glanced down at the card before replying, "Yes. Will you be there?"

Curiosity swept him as he realized he knew nothing about Nychelle Cory other than the fact she was intelligent, beautiful and a wonderful nurse. Was she married? He didn't think so. But he'd avoided asking too many questions about his colleagues and the staff, preferring them to volunteer whatever information they wanted him to have.

"Couldn't miss it." Her lips twisted briefly. "My life wouldn't be worth living if I did."

She must have seen the confusion in his eyes, because she waggled an index finger toward the invitation.

"My mother is chairperson this year. She'd have my guts for garters if I didn't turn up."

"Ah…"

Now he remembered where he'd heard Dr. Girvan's name before. Dr. H had advised him not to miss the gala, and had given him a rundown on some of the people he'd meet there. Dr. Girvan—Head of Psychiatry at the prestigious Brevard University Medical School—had definitely come up as a force to be reckoned with both in the medical and the wider communities.

"I've been dreading it a little, to be honest," he said, giving the card a flick of his finger. "I haven't been in Florida long enough to get to know many people and, frankly, any event where I have to wear a tuxedo is almost guaranteed to make me break out in hives."

Nychelle's laugh told him she didn't believe him for a moment. "I bet you'll fit right in. And there'll be a number of doctors from the clinic there, including Dr. H, so you'll know some people."

"Including you."

She dropped her gaze for a moment and he wondered what she was thinking. Then she looked up again, and he still had no idea what was going on in her head. It was as though she'd intentionally wiped her face clean of all expression.

"Including me."

"Do you have a date?"

As the impulsive words left his mouth David felt himself go still, waiting for her response.

"Um…no. I don't." She was rubbing her left wrist with her right hand, and then abruptly stopped, both hands going still in her lap.

Why was that a relief? He didn't want to know, really—was still wondering in the back of his mind exactly what the heck he was doing. Of all the people to ask to accompany him anywhere, Nychelle Cory was the worst possible choice.

Yet, as though from a distance, he heard himself ask, "Would you go with me?"

Surprise had her blinking at David as he continued, "I'd appreciate not having to walk into the gala by myself."

The one question that immediately reverberated in her head was, *Why?*

Why was he asking her to go with him when he could have his pick of women? Was it because he'd found out her mother was chairing the prestigious function? Perhaps he had even heard of her father who, as head of a world-renowned cardiac institute, also wielded considerable clout in the medical world? She knew what it felt like to have someone use her in an attempt to advance their medical career, and it was a situation she'd promised herself never to get into again.

Not wanting him to see how conflicted she was, Nychelle looked back down at the invitation, avoiding his gaze. How easy it was to remember Nick sucking up to her parents. She'd thought it was because he wanted to make a good impression. It was only later she'd realized he was only with her to get close to them—especially her father—hoping to worm his way into a position at the institute. There was no way she could trust David not to try something similar.

And, even without the fact she didn't want to be used

that way again, going with David to the gala would be stupid. There was something about him that drew her, excited her, and in her heart she knew staying away from him was definitely the best course of action. Being coolly professional over the last few days had been difficult enough, and just today, in the face of his obvious unhappiness, she'd so easily lost that clinical distance. Spending the evening with him seemed like pushing her luck too far.

No, she couldn't take the chance on any of it, so she replied in as expressionless a tone as she could manage. "I'm not sure that would be a good idea. It might lead to gossip here at the clinic."

David seemed to consider that for a moment, and when the silence had lasted longer than she'd expected, she finally looked up.

Meeting her gaze, he shook his head and held up one finger. "First, we're colleagues. Colleagues go to functions together all the time. It'll be more like carpooling." Another finger went up to emphasize his next point. "Second, I'd be happy to tell anyone who asks that you're doing me a good turn since I don't know that many people here yet." One last finger. "Third, if anyone comes to me trying to stir up trouble I'll tear a strip off them." Dropping his hand, he concluded, "I don't think it'll be a problem."

Damn him, those eyes made her just melt. About to press her palm to an overwarm cheek, she arrested the motion and lowered her hand back to her lap.

Maybe it wasn't such a bad idea after all. Perhaps seeing him currying favor with her parents would put an end to this silly attraction she felt. While her mother would take any deference as her due, her father, for all his status, seemed to thrive on being fawned on. Nychelle couldn't think of anything worse than watching David Warmington stroke their egos. It would immediately make him *persona non grata* in her book.

Tightening her lips, she gave in to the determined look in his eyes and nodded. It seemed wise, though, to qualify what they were doing. Make sure he knew it wasn't a date.

"Okay. Since you put it that way, I'll go with you. I don't like going to these functions solo either, so really you're doing me as much of a favor as I'm doing you."

"Great."

The corners of his lips twitched in one of his abbreviated smiles and Nychelle had to look away. Every time he did that she—ridiculously—just wanted to kiss him. Going with him seemed a worse and worse idea with each passing minute.

"Let me have your address and I'll pick you up," he added.

Without looking back up at him, she reached into the pocket of her lab coat and pulled out a pad. "I have to be there in time for the reception, so pick me up by six at the latest." She quickly scribbled down her address. "Do you know South Fort Lauderdale at all, or do you need directions?"

"I'll use my GPS. I'm sure I'll find it. But give me your phone number too, just in case."

Jotting down her home and cell phone numbers, she realized her heart rate was through the roof, as though from a shot of epinephrine. She tore the sheet off the pad and took a deep breath.

Then, reaching out to give him the paper, she forced her mind back to work and said, "I'm just following up on Mr. Comstock—letting you know he left here telling everyone what a brilliant doctor you are and promising to do his best…"

Yet, despite her carrying on a perfectly professional conversation regarding their mutual patient, one thought was paramount in her mind.

I'm going to have *to get a new dress!*

CHAPTER SIX

SEATED IN THE passenger seat of David's sedan, waiting for him to come around and open the door for her, Nychelle tried not to fidget with her hair or smooth down her dress.

Her wildly expensive, extravagant dress.

The kind of dress she usually never, ever bought but in this case hadn't been able to resist.

Nothing at any of the shops she usually patronized—most of which sold designer garments at reduced prices—had seemed appropriate. Finally she'd given in and gone to a boutique Aliya had once taken her to, where price sticker shock had almost caused her to have a heart attack. Right in the middle of the store, displayed in pride of place, she'd found *the dress* and, despite wanting to cry when she heard the price, she'd known it was perfect. After all, she was going to the gala with a man who just might be the best-looking one there. The last thing she wanted was to feel frumpy in comparison—especially in front of her parents.

Made of luxurious silk, with an intricate side-pleated, strapless bodice that fit her like a glove, and from which flowed a swirling, clingy skirt, the dress was two shades lighter than David's eyes. Looking at herself in the mirror, she'd felt beautiful, even sophisticated, and the appreciation in David's gaze when she'd opened her front door to him had been the icing on the cake. Having a gorgeous man solemnly tell you how beautiful you looked was an ego-booster, although she sternly cautioned herself not to take it to heart.

Now, as he swung the car door open and held out his hand, she steeled herself for the night ahead.

"Have I told you how lovely you look?" he asked, keeping hold of her hand although she was already out of the car.

"This makes three times." Slanting him a look, she reminded herself they weren't on a date one more time, and wriggled her fingers to try to make him let them go.

Instead of releasing her hand, David simply slid it up into the crook of his elbow, holding it there.

"Only three?" The corner of his mouth quirked, as he started leading her into the hotel. "I'm lagging behind... need to up my game. It should be at least a dozen times by now."

She had never thought she'd laugh while about to be subjected to her family in a formal professional setting, but somehow David managed it with his dry delivery.

"So, what am I in for tonight?"

They were crossing the lobby toward the banquet hall as he leaned in close to ask the question, his breath warm against her cheek.

"Will the food be good, or will I need to take you to a burger joint afterward?"

That made her giggle again, and it wasn't until they were right at the door that she realized her stomach wasn't tied in knots the way it usually was before one of these events.

"Nychelle—glad you could make it on time." Her mother gave her a perfunctory hug and the obligatory air-kiss near one cheek, before adding, "And you took time to find something suitable to wear."

"Yes, Mom."

Ugh. That lukewarm reception knocked a lot of the wind out of her sails, leaving Nychelle caught somewhere between annoyance and disappointment. And, even though she wanted to see David's demeanor as she introduced him, she was too embarrassed by her mother's greeting to look at his face.

"Mom, I don't think you've met Dr. David Warmington? David, this is my mother, Dr. Monique Girvan."

The look of quickly disguised shock on her mother's face when she realized Nychelle had a date should have made Nychelle want to laugh, but it only served to make her feel that much worse.

"A pleasure to meet you, Dr. Warmington." Back to her usual urbane self, her mom gave David one of her piercing, interrogatory looks. "Dr. Hamatty has mentioned you. So nice of you to come—and to give Nychelle a ride."

"The pleasure is all mine, Dr. Girvan. On all fronts."

Nychelle thought there was a hint of coolness in his greeting and glanced up. Although he was smiling, the expression didn't reach his eyes.

"Your daughter was kind enough to agree to accompany me, and my appreciation for that knows no bounds."

Then they were moving forward, and Nychelle was greeting the next person in the receiving line, and whatever her mother said in reply to David was lost in the murmur of voices.

Once they'd cleared the line Nychelle glanced around, still stung by her mother's attitude, looking everywhere but at David.

"They've really outdone themselves with the decor this year. Those arrangements of calla lilies and orchids are amazing." She was babbling, and she knew it, but somehow couldn't stop. "Did you get a chance to check out the items up for auction? They should have sent you a list with the invitation. There are some gorgeous paintings, and a sculpture I absolutely covet..."

Warm fingers closed around her wrist, stemming the

flow of words spilling from her mouth, and when she glanced up David's intent expression made her breath hitch. Then he was leaning close, his cheek almost resting against hers, and the scent of expensive cologne and heated male caused a cascade of goose bumps over her arms and back.

"I don't care how old you are. If you were my daughter the last thing I'd call that dress is *'appropriate.'*"

His fingers, somehow both firm and gentle at the same time, skimmed up her arm to her shoulder, stopping just shy of her collarbone, and a sweet shiver traveled up her spine.

"It's alluring. Decadent. Deliciously sensual. It'll make every red-blooded man in this room want to take it off."

His hand fell away. That simple touch had left her far more aroused than it should have been able to. Made her want to grab his hand and pull it back, guide it lower, to where her breast swelled over the bodice of the dress in question.

"Highly inappropriate from a parental point of view, I would have thought."

The right response would be to laugh, make light of what he was saying, but her insides were at war. She was dry-mouthed, her heartbeat threatening to go completely out of control. Taking a deep breath made it worse, because David was still leaning close and that scent, which she found excessively sexy, filled her already swimming head.

Then he straightened. "I'm going to have to beat the men off you tonight, aren't I?" He said it in a wry, conversational tone, but his lips twitched, revealing his amusement. "Good thing I've been going to the gym."

Trust him to make her smile, even when it was the last thing she felt like doing. Gathering her composure, she slanted him a glance, then quickly looked away again, because the warmth in his eyes was threatening to undo all her hard-won poise.

"Oh, I think we'll be okay. Everyone tends to be on their best behavior at these galas."

Tucking her fingers into the crook of his arm again, David muttered, "Darn it. I suppose I'll have be too, then. Just my luck." Then, before she could do more than chuckle, he continued, "Come on—let's take a stroll around and look at the auction items. I want to see this sculpture you like so much."

And she was happy to comply, knowing the night probably wouldn't get any better.

Dinner had been delicious—far better than he'd expected from past experience—and the after-dinner speeches hadn't droned on and on, as they so often did at these affairs. And being seated at a table with four other doctors from the Lauderlakes clinic, along with their accompanying spouses and significant others, had ensured pleasant dinner conversation, without any of the awkwardness that would have come with sitting with strangers.

And, of course, there was Nychelle—who had taken his breath away when she'd opened her front door earlier, and continued to do so every time he looked at her. At least here he had the opportunity to watch her openly, instead of surreptitiously as he often found himself doing at the clinic. Truth be told, tonight he'd had to tear his gaze away periodically, since the temptation was to hang on to her every word and gesture like a doofus.

Or some kind of creepy stalker.

He really wasn't sure which one was accurate, but at least he was able to acknowledge it was one or the other and rein himself in. It shouldn't be this difficult. They weren't on a date, and he didn't want it to be one.

At the time, asking her to come with him had seemed like a great idea. He liked her, found her good company, and got the impression she wasn't particularly interested in him other than as a colleague and perhaps a casual friend. That last fact made her the perfect companion, so any problems he had were squarely on him.

Despite his fascination with Nychelle, and the spurt of annoyance he'd felt with the way her mother greeted her, from David's point of view it had been a great evening.

Until now, when they were mingling with the other attendees. In particular, standing and chatting with Nychelle's father.

When first introduced to the older man, David had been struck by the similarities in looks and deportment between father and daughter, and had been inclined to like the man just on that basis. Now he was wondering how such a cool and pompous man could have produced the warm and friendly Nychelle.

"Nychelle would have made a competent doctor if she'd had the ambition." Dr. Herman Cory paused to take a sip from the glass in his hand. "Unfortunately she refused to listen to career advice from her mother and me. Luckily her sister makes up for it."

Annoyed, David lifted his glass to his lips just so he wouldn't have to reply to Dr. Cory's comment. Glancing at Nychelle, he saw a half smile tipping her lips, but zero amusement in her eyes. However, she didn't look surprised at the fact her father was singing her sister's praises and had been for the last five minutes straight. Apparently it wasn't anything new.

"Olivia was in the top five percentile in all her courses, and before she even graduated she was being headhunted by the Mayo Clinic and John Hopkins."

Unable to stand it a moment longer, David replied, "It must be very satisfying to have two such intelligent and talented daughters."

Dr. Cory waved his hand—somewhat dismissively,

David thought. “Of course. It’s just a shame Nychelle isn’t living up to her full potential.”

“I disagree.”

If the circumstances had been different, he’d have been amused at the older man’s obvious surprise at being so clearly contradicted. As it was, Dr. Cory’s arched eyebrows just added to David’s annoyance.

“I have no doubt Nychelle would make an excellent doctor, in any specialty she chose, but as a nurse practitioner she’s fulfilling a vital role at our clinic, and she is one of the very best diagnosticians I’ve come across, whether doctor or nurse.”

The noise Dr. Cory made in the back of his throat didn’t bode well for the direction the conversation was about to take, and David braced himself.

“Being a nurse practitioner is all well and good, but it certainly isn’t the same as being a doctor.”

“Of course it isn’t.” David tried to smile, but it probably looked more like a snarl. “In many ways it’s better. The move we’ve made away from the ‘cradle to grave’ style of medicine, where a family doctor knows his patients over the long term, necessitates people like Nychelle. She can and does take the time to get to know the patients and their histories, without costing the same amount as a doctor would. Without her, and others like her, many more patients would fall through the cracks, or be diagnosed with diseases too late for the doctors to do anything for them.”

Dr. Cory drew himself up to his full height. “It doesn’t change the fact that Nychelle has wasted the opportunity she had to excel in the medical field. If she wanted to be a clinician, then she should have gone to medical school and become a general practitioner. As a father, I find her choices untenable.”

Taking a deep breath and a sip of his drink bought David enough time to control his close to boiling temper.

Once he was assured he wasn't about to say something he'd regret later, he replied, "Not to put too fine a point on it, sir, but it seems to me your daughter *has* excelled in the medical field. If she weren't the best of the best in her specialty I doubt Dr. Hamatty would have hired her, or given her the level of responsibility she has. I think most fathers would be ecstatic to have her as a daughter."

Silence fell between the three of them, leaving David to wonder if he'd totally overstepped the bounds of politeness the way he feared. Didn't the man know how lucky he was to have Nychelle? It was infuriating to see that Dr. Cory was so focused on his own wishes he couldn't even appreciate the joy of fatherhood, much less be proud of the wonderful woman Nychelle had grown into.

What David wouldn't give for the opportunity to see his daughter growing into a woman. He wouldn't care what career she chose, as long as she was a good and decent person like Nychelle.

He had the urge to look at Nychelle, to see if she was angry with him, but instead he kept his gaze fixed on her father, willing the stubborn man to concede at least that to his daughter.

"Hey, Nychelle. How are you?"

The interruption, caused by a tall, handsome, dark-skinned man, who bent to hug and kiss Nychelle before turning to shake Dr. Cory's hand, was welcomed—by David at least. Also by Nychelle, if her smile was any indication.

"Martin. I was wondering where you and Jennifer were." She turned to hug the short blonde woman who'd been a step behind the man. "Jennifer. Good to see you." Then she waved a hand in David's direction. "Have you two met Dr. David Warmington? David, this is my cousin, Dr. Martin Girvan, and his wife, Dr. Jennifer Howard."

"I do believe I have."

When Martin Girvan turned to shake David's hand, a big smile on his thin face, his eyes twinkling from behind thick glasses, David felt a trickle of recognition.

"The New York conference on the international transmission of vector-borne diseases."

"Yes, of course." David felt some of the tension ease from the back of his neck at the other man's warm reception and at the knowledge that, hopefully, the conversation he'd just been engaged in was now over. "Nice to see you again."

"And you." Martin threw an arm over his diminutive wife's shoulders and pulled her closer. "Jen, this is the doctor I told you about—the one who saved me from an uncomfortable situation with a rather tipsy gentleman in the hotel bar."

David laughed, remembering the incident in question. "I was just glad we were both able to get away unscathed."

"Are you working in Florida now? I remember you being elsewhere at the time..."

"I was in Chicago. Now I'm at the Lauderlakes clinic."

"Ah." Martin smiled. "Snapped up by Dr. Hamatty, eh? And I assume that's where you met Nychelle?"

All three of them—David, Martin and Jennifer—turned toward where Nychelle had been standing, but she was gone.

Looking over her cousin's shoulder, David saw her slipping out of the ballroom and with a quick, "Excuse me," went after her.

CHAPTER SEVEN

SHE SHOULD BE used to it by now, and in many ways she was, yet tonight her parents' attitude toward her and her work—her life—stung worse than ever.

For them to speak to and about her like that, in front of a man who not only was a stranger to them but also her colleague, had Nychelle seething in a maelstrom of anger and embarrassment.

As she made her way quickly through the hotel lobby toward the open terrace doors on the other side, she tried to unclench her fists and keep a pleasant expression on her face.

It was so hard.

Her father denigrated her so casually, as though nothing she'd worked for and achieved had any value. Oh, she knew it was what he thought—he'd made it known *ad nauseam*. But somehow tonight it had sounded worse than usual. Made her *feel* worse than usual. Not even reminding herself why she'd made the choices she had, and how close she was to fulfilling one of her most dearly held dreams, took away the hurt and sense of isolation.

Nychelle had long ago recognized her parents' seeming inability to offer any kind of affection, knowing their every thought regarding their children was focused solely on career paths and advancement. She wasn't built that way.

Never had been. Oh, as a child she'd tried desperately to be what they wanted, constantly striving for perfection in the hope of getting positive attention from them. It had been soul-destroying—especially as she'd grown older and realized what they wanted her to be was vastly different from who she wanted to be.

Everything had changed when she was thirteen, and had been diagnosed with dysfunctional uterine bleeding. A D&C had been her final course of treatment, and the doctor had warned that conception might prove difficult later on, because of the scarring left on her uterus.

But it wasn't the diagnosis that had caused her change of perspective; it had been her mother's response to hearing it. Coldly and clinically, she'd expressed a kind of satisfaction. It was the perfect reason for Nychelle to concentrate completely on a career in medicine. There would be none of the potential stumbling blocks or distractions children often caused.

Nychelle shook her head, still unable to comprehend how such a well-regarded psychiatrist could have so little understanding of her own offspring. It was one of the universe's great mysteries.

Maneuvering around a cluster of people near the doors, she slipped past and out into the warm night air. The long terrace was dotted with folks, many of whom were familiar to Nychelle. Hopefully keeping her gaze distant and her steps brisk, as though she was on her way somewhere important, would deter anyone inclined to speak to her. She really needed a little solitude to get her temper under control.

Near the middle of the terrace, some steps led down to a boardwalk above the sand at the ocean's edge. Reaching them, she swerved to descend toward the beach, quickly leaving the lights of the patio behind as she went.

As soon as she was alone, she tilted her head back and released the sigh of anger and pain she'd been holding inside toward the full moon above, trying to let the sound of the water soothe her.

She'd tried so hard to get to a place of acceptance where her parents were concerned, but it was an ongoing battle—one she feared she'd never win and, as a result, often considered giving up on. They didn't even attempt to understand her—why should she bother trying to understand and be tolerant of them? They might be at the top of their fields professionally, but as parents they were, in her book, dismal failures. They'd let her down and embarrassed her once again.

It all made her want to pound her fists on the wooden railing in front of her, but instead she took a deep breath. As she exhaled she tried to relax, but the memory of her father's words kept digging at her, tightening her muscles.

Yet it also could be taken as another indication that she was doing the right thing. A sign that being married, or even in a long-term relationship before having children, was highly overrated. Her parents might have been married for almost thirty-five years, but they spoke to each other with the coolness of strangers. They treated their children as though they were ongoing work projects, rather than individuals whose particular talents and desires should be nurtured.

Once upon a time Nychelle had hoped to find a soul mate, a partner in every respect of the word, but having given her all to Nick, only to be completely betrayed, she'd given up that dream. No. She knew she had what it took to give her children everything they needed without any help. And if her parents ever tried to embarrass her children the way her father had just done to her, making someone else—virtually a stranger—feel it necessary to come to their defense…

She let out a little growl.

Thank goodness for Martin and Jennifer interrupting

before her father had had a chance to answer David. Dr. Herman Cory, head of the world-renowned Maynard Heart Institute, wasn't used to being challenged and didn't like it one little bit. In fact, Nychelle would go so far as to say he hated it. And David had definitely thrown down the gauntlet.

A little smile broke through her anger at the memory. When last had anyone, even herself, stood up in defense of her life like that? She couldn't remember. It showed David wasn't intimidated by her parents, or out to worm his way into their good graces, and it made her like him all the more.

"I like you a lot, Nychelle, and I already think of you as a friend. But I have to be honest. Your dad is a piece of work."

The sound of David's voice was startling. She'd been so wrapped up in her thoughts she hadn't heard him approach, and she was too embarrassed to face him.

"That he is."

Trying to inject even a veneer of amusement into her voice was difficult, and she wasn't sure she'd managed it. Keeping her gaze fixed on the creamy disc of the moon rising over the water, she continued, "My parents are both overachievers and they raised my sister and me to be the same. It irks them that I went my own way rather than follow the path they planned out for me."

David's chuckle was warm, as was the hand he cupped over the curve of her shoulder. "I understand. In a strange way, although our situations are very different, they're also remarkably similar."

Oh, Dr. Heat was living up to his name, if the little licks of flaming awareness tickling over the skin of her arm were anything to go by. The attraction she felt was impossible to ignore, but she had to disregard it. For her own sanity, if nothing else.

Yet she was unable to resist the lure of his voice and,

wanting to see his face, tilted her head to look at him over her shoulder. Even with just the glow of moonlight, she was effortlessly trapped by his gaze, and it was a struggle to ask, "How so?"

"I come from a poor family. The town where I grew up was once a thriving mining center, but steadily declined over the years. My parents expected me to learn a trade—preferably become a mechanic so I could eventually take over my father's shop. Imagine their shock when I decided I wanted to study medicine."

There was a flash of his abbreviated smile, but there was genuine sadness behind it.

"I was ten when I first mentioned it, and they were horrified. No one in my family had ever gone to college, much less to med school. I don't think they knew what to make of me. They still don't."

Dragging her gaze from his, she nodded, seeing the correlation—although to her mind it was tenuous. "I guess it all boils down to unmet expectations."

"Exactly."

His fingers tightened on her shoulder, just enough to bring her full awareness of them, and then relaxed.

"Our parents expected us to follow in their footsteps but we decided to forge our own course. None of them is comfortable with that, even though we're successful and, I think, we've both turned out okay."

"And not even, in my case, when they have another child happily following the life plan they laid out."

The spurt of annoyance she experienced as she spoke was swiftly swamped by the sensation of his fingers soothingly tracing along the skin of her upper arm. It was impossible to continue speaking, and she was glad when David replied so she didn't have to say anything more.

"Mine too." David chuckled again.

A shiver of desire raced up her spine, and she barely heard him continue.

"My sister, Mary-Elizabeth, works with my dad now, and my little brother, Donny, is just about to get his master mechanic's ticket. The family business is in good hands. But I want you to understand something..."

She waited for him to go on, trying to control the tremors fluttering in her belly. During the conversation he'd moved closer, and now his scent and heat, and the sheer sexiness of his voice, seemed to envelop her, ramping up the waves of arousal washing through her blood.

"I didn't say what I did to your father for any reason other than I believe every word."

His hand slid back up to her shoulder, and before she realized what he was planning he'd turned her to face him.

"You're an amazing person. You excel at your job and you make the clinic so much more efficient than it could ever be without you. On top of that, you make the entire place brighter just with your personality. Any father would be proud and happy to have such an incredible daughter. If your father can't appreciate how lucky he is, that's his loss."

Gratitude and something deeper, more intense, tightened her chest. His tone, matter-of-fact and sincere, made tears prickle behind her eyelids.

"Thank you."

It was little more than a whisper, and instinctively she reached up to kiss his cheek, wanting to express in some tangible way how much she valued his words.

When her lips touched his skin, all the sounds of the party, the calling of the nocturnal frogs, even the wash and retreat of the waves faded. As though struck to stone, neither of them moved for a long moment, and then, with what sounded suspiciously like a curse, David turned his head and their mouths met.

A shock like hundreds of volts of electricity jolted

through her at the first firm, delicious touch of his lips—and then everything stopped.

Her breath caught somewhere deep in her chest.

The racing of her heart stilled.

The world, the universe, seemed concentrated on that one stunning point of contact between them.

Then David was holding her, one hand on her nape, the other around her waist, pulling her close, and her body shuddered into hyperawareness, her heart galloping, breath rushing. With a light sweep his tongue requested entrance to her mouth and she opened for him instinctively, gladly. A rumble vibrated from his chest, through his lips and into hers, causing a cascade of sensation so intense Nychelle trembled from head to toe. Putting her arms around his neck was not only a way to get closer but also necessary to stop herself from melting into a puddle at his feet.

With each of her rushed inhalations came his scent, excitingly familiar and yet different, more intimate. Beneath her hands his shoulders flexed and, being held so close to his chest, she not only heard but felt the escalation of his breathing.

Need crashed through every cell of her body, bringing her nipples to tight, aching buds and causing yearning to bloom deep in her belly. It was more than mere craving. It was agonizing want, and it tore a gasp from her throat.

As though in response to that telling sound, David deepened the kiss. Nychelle pressed even closer, lost in the power of the desire building between them, which threatened to overwhelm her completely. David shifted, bringing one muscular thigh to rest between her legs, and as she felt his erection against her Nychelle arched into the contact, suddenly desperate for more—more of him, more of these out-of-control yet, oh, so decadent feelings.

His lips slid from hers, tracing a path along her jaw to the sensitive flesh below her ear.

"Nychelle..."

How had she never heard her name said that way before? As though it were the most beautiful word ever created? As though it were the code to unlock the door leading to every fantasy of fulfillment she'd ever had? Just the sound of it made her head fall back, baring her throat for the onslaught of his lips.

"Yes," he growled, before taking advantage of what she offered and kissing down the tendons straining in her neck.

"Ahhh..." A soft, moaning sigh broke from her as those firm, determined lips found her collarbone. Already she was anticipating them on her breasts, imagining the pleasure as he kissed lower, and then lower still.

A burst of laughter came from the terrace above, loud enough to break through the fiery bubble of lust they were cocooned in, and they both stiffened.

"I think the waiter said they only allow smoking at the end of the boardwalk, so if you want to smoke those stinky cigars that's where you'll have to go."

The woman's voice carried clearly through the night air, but it took a moment for Nychelle's befuddled mind to understand what she was saying.

Once she did, reality came crashing down, and she pushed David away as hard as she could.

Realizing they were about to have company, David cursed under his breath, and he had already started straightening when Nychelle's hands found his chest and gave him a hard shove. Stepping back, he held on to her long enough to make sure she didn't lose her balance, and then let go as though touching her burned his palms.

In truth, Nychelle had brought to life an inferno with her kisses. *Shocked* didn't begin to describe how he felt about the instant devastating arousal just the touch of her lips had created. The intensity of his desire for her had awoken something deep inside him. Awakened needs so long suppressed he'd thought they'd completely died.

And everything about the emotions coursing through his veins told him it was so right as to be completely wrong.

He couldn't afford to chance getting seriously involved again. The pain of losing Natalie and the destruction of his marriage as a result of that loss had left him damaged in a fundamental way. Desire was fine, but what he felt now seemed to go crazily beyond that into the danger zone.

He didn't want to take the chance of losing another child, so he'd long ago decided it was better not to put himself in a position where it might happen. He'd only just gotten to know Nychelle, but somehow, deep inside, he sensed she posed a threat to all the decisions he'd made about his life going forward.

They stared at each other, and she seemed poised to dash away.

Forcing a deep breath into his lungs, he gathered all the calm he could muster. He needed to get her back at arm's length.

"I suppose I should apologize."

He was proud of how cool he sounded, even with his heart still crashing against his ribs.

"It was an impulse—probably brought on by the moonlight."

Nychelle blinked, then looked up at the moon. "No, it was my fault for—"

"Look," he interrupted, not wanting to prolong what might turn into a painful conversation. "I think the best thing is for us to just pretend none of this happened."

He only just stopped a bitter bark of laughter from escaping. He'd suggested it, but in reality it would be easier to stop the moon from orbiting Earth than to forget the sensation of her body and her mouth, hot and eager, pressed to his.

"That's a good idea."

He heard her inhale and then let the air out with a *whoosh.*

"It shouldn't have happened. We work together. Situations like this can cause so many problems, make life difficult at the clinic, even threaten my career."

Her tone was brisk—the one she often used with patients or other members of staff. It wasn't offensive at all, but each time she used it David could hear her putting distance between herself and the person she was talking to.

He tried to tamp down his irritation at her eager acquiescence. Wasn't he the one who'd suggested they forget it?

Gritting his teeth at his own contrariness, he replied, "I completely understand what you mean. Too much of a risk for something as unimportant as one kiss shared in the moonlight."

He thought she tensed for a moment, but then she relaxed again before replying, "Exactly."

Desperate to bring some sort of normality back to their evening, he said the first thing that came into his still muddled head. "Glad to know my lunacy hasn't chased you away."

"Ha-ha-ha." She brushed her hands over the front of her dress, as though making sure it hadn't become disarrayed during their embrace. "So many studies say the supposed increase in incidents needing police or medical intervention during the full moon is just anecdotal, but when I worked in the ER it sure seemed real."

"When I was doing my clinical residency in Chicago it seemed real to me too." Unable to resist, he touched her arm, guiding her back toward the steps leading to the terrace. "There was always an increase in patients being admitted from the emergency room the day after a full moon."

Near to the steps, and in the pool of light shining down from the terrace above, he paused. It felt wrong to leave things the way they were.

"By the way, I want to thank you again for agreeing to come with me tonight. Functions like this can be pretty awkward when you walk in alone."

Nychelle glanced at him, and David suddenly wished he had a way to capture how amazing she looked bathed in moonlight, made mysterious and otherworldly by the attendant shadows. Not that he'd ever forget it. No, these moments they'd shared would definitely stick with him, he was sure.

"You're welcome." Her brows dipped together for a moment. "I meant it when I said you were doing me as much of a favor as I was you."

There were shadows in her eyes, sadness in the set of her lips, and the memory of her mother's lukewarm greeting and her father's denial of her worth made anger spurt through him once more.

Why couldn't they see how wonderful Nychelle truly was?

The impulse to see her smile again was irresistible, and without thinking it through he said, "Ha! Let's see if you still feel that way after I step on your toes a few times on the dance floor."

Her delicious giggle eased something in his belly, but he was kicking himself. So much for keeping her at arm's length… At least for tonight.

CHAPTER EIGHT

THE MONDAY AFTER the gala dawned clear and warm, a typically beautiful Florida day, but Nychelle had to drag herself out of bed. Yawning prodigiously, she contemplated whether to forgo her usual yoga workout. She thought she'd slept fairly well, once she'd actually got her brain to shut up long enough for her to doze off, but her bone-deep weariness seemed to indicate otherwise. Pushing herself to exercise seemed the right thing to do, and she felt somewhat revived by the time she got into her car to go to work.

Yet in the back of her mind the events of Saturday night kept swirling, just as they had all Sunday. It seemed as though her brain was caught in a loop, replaying the kiss she'd shared with David over and over. And every time she thought about it waves of hot and cold chased each other through her body.

Oh, she had no doubt he regretted it had happened; he'd made that crystal-clear with his reaction and the cold way he'd told her to forget it. That was good advice. She just wished she could follow it as easily as she'd agreed to do so.

Besides, she must have been crazy, giving in to his kisses like that. There was no room in her life for that kind of nonsense—especially with a man who seemed able to turn off his emotions so easily. Just because he hadn't made any attempt to impress her parents didn't mean she could trust him. Getting burned by Nick was more than enough embarrassment for one lifetime.

As she made the turn off the highway a couple blocks from the office she realized she was grinding her teeth, and forced herself to stop. By the end of the day the entire building would know she had gone to the gala with Dr. Heat. If she wanted to retain any sanity she was going to have to convince everyone they were just friends, even with the memory of his embrace refusing to go away.

After climbing out of the car at the office, she slammed the door closed a little harder than was strictly necessary.

Gina, of course, cornered her almost before Nychelle had a chance to put on her lab coat.

"You sneaky thing, you. I heard you were at the FMA gala with Dr. Heat. Why didn't you mention you were going on a date with him?"

Nychelle pulled her head out of the supply locker to give the other woman a bland look. "It wasn't a date—more of a mutual favor. He didn't have anyone to go with, and neither did I." Then she smiled, which at least came naturally. "You should have seen my mother's face when I walked in with him. That was definitely worth the price of admission."

Gina looked disappointed, but then perked up again almost immediately. "Did he make a pass at you?"

"Nah." Thank goodness she'd gone back to gathering the samples her office was low on, so Gina couldn't see her face. "He was a perfect gentleman."

The sound Gina made was filled with a mixture of disapproval and disappointment, and it made Nychelle snicker. Then the receptionist moved a little closer, and whispered, "That's crazy. Do you think he's gay?"

"What? No!" Nychelle glared at the other woman. "I'm sure he isn't. It's just that..." She remembered how David had convinced her to go with him, and grabbed onto the words like a lifeline. "We work together. It was more like…um…carpooling than anything else."

"Huh." Gina tossed her head. "Well, I guess it's not a bad thing, really, that he behaved himself. But, *sheesh*, I'd have thought—"

"You're too much for me this morning, girl." Nychelle forced a laughing tone into her voice, thankful there were only a few more minutes before the clinic officially opened. "I've got to get going."

Gina glanced at her watch. "Gosh, yes. Me too."

Nychelle sighed as the receptionist walked away. Hopefully the rest of the day wasn't going to be more of the same.

It wasn't as bad as she'd expected—mainly because the clinic was so busy. Which was why she was so surprised to notice that all the appointments after three o'clock were gone from her schedule. When she buzzed through to the medical office assistant who handled her schedule she was told Dr. Hamatty's assistant had called down and asked for it to be done, and couldn't stop a little spurt of anxiety.

"Did she say why?"

"No, Nurse Cory. She just said there was to be a meeting at three Dr. H. wanted you involved in, and told me to clear you for the rest of the day."

Unusual, but she refused to get herself worked up until she knew there was a good reason for it. "Where's the meeting?"

"In your office."

The woman sounded harried, and Nychelle could hear phones ringing in the background. The questions flying around in her head would just have to wait, apparently.

"Okay, Marion. Has my next patient arrived yet?"

By two-forty-five her last patient had left and Nychelle had entered her notes into the records system, which gave her plenty of time before the meeting. More than enough to have her once more wondering what it was all about.

Encircling her right wrist with the fingers of her left hand, she convulsively twisted it back and forth—a nervous habit she'd had from when she was a young child. Why was she so on edge? Lauderlakes was a busy, vibrant place, and special projects and situations arose all the time. There really was no need to be this tense about an unexpected meeting, but she'd been as jumpy as a flea since the gala.

Telling herself it was because she would know within a few days whether the IUI had been successful or not didn't quell the nervous flutters in her stomach. Maybe because she was honest enough to admit that wasn't the entire reason.

She took a deep breath, trying to ease the rush of sensations firing through her body, but didn't succeed.

Despite not trusting him, she'd found herself building fantasies, both sexual and otherwise, around David when her entire attention should be on the future she was trying to create for herself. All her emotional energy needed to be focused on the life she hoped was growing inside her—not on a man who had clearly stated he wasn't interested in fatherhood.

Perhaps she was using him as a distraction—a way to not have to concentrate on Wednesday and the tests her obstetrician would have run by then. That was hopefully the day she'd start planning her life as a mother. She had no time to waste on David Warmington.

Luckily, she had no reason to see him very much going forward, other than in passing here at the clinic. After the kiss they'd shared, which neither had mentioned again once they'd gone back inside to the gala, he'd been the perfect gentleman. Polite. Polished. Amusing.

And subtly distant.

While she'd appreciated all the former attributes, that last one had stung. Which annoyed her no end. It was what she wanted, right? In fact, what she needed. It should have put her at ease, erased the heightened awareness she felt in his presence—not left her still shivery and aroused, flustered and unhappy. The unreasonableness of her reaction annoyed her even more.

It was definitely time to put all that behind her and concentrate on going forward the way she'd planned—including making sure her work here at the clinic was exemplary. This was a job she intended to keep for a very long time. Stability would be especially important when she became a single mother. In three months there'd be another free clinic, this time for adults, and because of the insane preparations necessary to make it a success the committee meetings started that evening.

Pulling up the list of first steps they'd compiled after much trial and error, Nychelle started going through it, making notes on what should be changed or adjusted. She was so immersed in her chore, it was only when the intercom buzzed that she realized it was already ten minutes past three.

"Yes, Marion?"

"Dr. Warmington is here for you, Nurse Cory."

What? David? Why?

Thankfully, professionalism was so deeply ingrained in her character she didn't say the words aloud, even though they'd risen into her suddenly dry throat.

Knowing her silence was on the verge of becoming ridiculous, she said, "Send him in, please, Marion."

David blew in through the door, giving Nychelle only a couple of moments to gather her wits and arrange her expression into a mildly surprised one.

"Sorry I'm late," he said, as soon as he was in her office. "I just finished a meeting with Dr. Hamatty."

Her heart rate, which had jumped when she'd heard David's name, ramped up a little more, but she kept her response to, "Oh? What's going on?"

He glanced at his watch and, although she waved a hand toward the visitor's chair on the other side of her desk, stayed on his feet.

"He's requested that you and I handle an off-site intake. The patient flew in today by private jet from New York, and we need to meet with her, receive her records from the medical team who flew in with her, and do an evaluation."

"Okay." It was a little unusual, although not unheard of. Some of the patients Lauderlakes attracted were extremely wealthy, and demanded special attention. "Where are we seeing the patient and what time do we need to get there?"

David gave her the address, while looking at his watch again. "The medical team has to leave by four thirty to get back to the airport, and since I'm not that familiar with the area I think we should leave immediately. I can fill you in on the way there."

The clipped tone and the way he hardly even glanced at her gave her the sense that whatever friendship they might have developed had evaporated. She wasn't sure whether to be angry or relieved—wasn't even sure what the achy feeling growing in her chest could be. So she ignored it, storing it away for later consideration. If he wanted a cool, professional relationship that was exactly what he'd get.

Nychelle turned the address over in her mind. "That's in Las Olas. I know the way, so I may as well drive." Without waiting for his reply, she added, "That way you can concentrate on bringing me up to speed on the patient without having to keep your eyes on the road."

By the time she'd finished speaking she already had her phone in her hand and had dialed. David's lips parted, but she held up one hand to forestall him when she heard Marion answer.

"Hey, I'm heading out for an off-site intake. If anyone asks, let them know I'll be back in time for the committee meeting this evening."

As she hung up the receiver David said, "I can drive and talk at the same time."

At any other time the disgruntled tone would have made her smile. Just now, though, she felt anything but amused by him. She stood up and made tracks for the door, striding right past him without even a sideways look.

"No doubt—but I'm driving anyway."

Then she walked out of the office without another word.

David didn't bother to argue with Nychelle. He knew that expression all too well. It was the same bland, don't-mess-with-me look his mother often got when she put her foot down about something. It was probably wisest not to complain—not even about Nychelle's sedan being so small he was forced to push the passenger seat all the way back to get enough leg room. The atmosphere was frosty enough without risking another layer of ice being added.

It was what he'd aimed for, wasn't it? This impersonal, professional distance? He knew that after that kiss they'd shared, and the erotic dreams he'd had about her since, dialing back their relationship was imperative. So why did he have this intense need to get back on friendly terms?

Nychelle drove the same way she did everything else—with smooth, calm competence. Turning out of the clinic parking lot, she went east for a while, and then turned south on Highway US1. She didn't seem at all perturbed by the silence that had fallen between them, and David rubbed the back of his neck, wondering why it was bothering him so much.

He found himself searching for something to say—something that would make her smile, or at least start talking to him in that easy, cheerful way she had.

"I'm surprised you drive a stick shift."

As the words left his mouth he had to swallow a groan of disgust. His comment bordered on insulting, and Nychelle seemed to think so too, if her response was anything to go by.

"I'm not sure why." There was that cool, uninterested tone again. "Why don't you tell me about the patient?"

The snub was deserved, although it made heat spread uncomfortably across his nape and up into his scalp.

Opening the small laptop, he cleared his throat, hoping to sound normal and professional—not to mention as cool as she did—while he spoke. "Twenty-year-old female, Carmen Fitzpatrick. Hemoglobin SS Sickle Cell Disease."

"In crisis?"

"Had one—" David checked the notes "—four days ago. She's a musician and was just coming off tour when the crisis occurred."

"Ah. Now I realize why her name sounded familiar. That's Carmie-K."

Surprised, he looked over at her. "You know her?"

Nychelle shrugged. "Just her music. She sings a fusion of rap, reggae, blues and soul. It's not bad, actually. And, before you ask why someone my age listens to her, Martin's kids love her music, and, after hearing it first through them, I do too."

He'd just gotten over his first round of embarrassment for the stick shift comment, and now she'd put him back on the spot.

"I'd never ask something like that."

Good grief, he sounded defensive even to his own ears, and Nychelle just pursed her lips, her gaze firmly on the road and the traffic around them, her expression both skeptical and annoyed.

He was racking his brain for an appropriate follow-up comment—one that would get him out of the doghouse—when she asked, "Did Dr. H mention why she was here in Fort Lauderdale? I got the impression that she lives in New York City."

While he was relieved at this return to business, David had to fight the urge to take the conversation back to a more personal level. He didn't want her thinking of him as some condescending idiot, but keeping the conversation on the patient was probably a good idea.

"She bought a house here a while back and planned to move here after the tour. I get the impression her hematologist in New York wasn't too happy about her making the trip, but she was determined."

Nychelle checked her rearview mirror before changing lanes. "Does she have a hematologist lined up here?"

"Yes. Dr. Yuen at Broward Health."

"And Lauderlakes is to be her primary health provider." It wasn't a question, but a statement. "Will she come in to the clinic after this, when she's feeling better, or will she want house calls going forward?"

"I don't know. That's something we'll have to discuss with her."

Nychelle had turned off US1 onto Las Olas Boulevard a while back. They'd passed a high-end commercial area, then gone over a bridge, and now she navigated a construction zone.

"She's notoriously private," she said in a thoughtful tone. "Leighann, Martin's daughter, is obsessed with Carmie-K but she's never said anything about her having sickle cell disease, so I don't think it's common knowledge. It would explain why she bought a house here, rather than in South Beach or Miami. Less chance of being stalked by the paparazzi."

"I wouldn't know about that." He was watching her profile, enjoying the opportunity to do so without it seeming weird. "Paparazzi are as far outside of my experience as traveling into space."

"Mine too, but I guess Carmie has to think about things like that. Remind me of the address."

She slowed down, and after reading it out to her David turned his attention to where they were going. One of the myriad canals that crisscrossed the city was on their left, and on their right were large houses, just visible behind high fences and verdant vegetation.

"Nice area," he said.

The houses were on what seemed to be a series of man-made peninsulas, separated by canals. Looking along the canals, he could see the backs of mansions with neat lawns flowing down to the water. Berthed behind most of the houses were boats of varying sizes—none of them dinghies, by any means.

"I didn't know this was here, but I haven't spent much time exploring the city."

"My parents live just down there."

She pointed to the road they were going past, and David looked. More mansions.

"Is it just the two of them?" Considering her parents' positions, he shouldn't be surprised, but he was. Part of him still found it difficult to reconcile what people had in comparison to what they needed. "Not to be rude, but I don't see any small homes around here. Isn't it a lot of house for just two?"

"Yep."

She sent him a sideways glance, and he thought there was a glint of amusement in her eyes. Seeing it made his neck and shoulder muscles suddenly relax, although he hadn't been aware of how tight they'd become.

"It's rather wasted on them—especially since neither of my parents like the sea, so they don't own a boat." She chuckled. "Not that you have to have a boat when you live on the water, but it makes sense. No, that house is a showplace for visitors and a giant, fancy peapod for the two of them to rattle around in."

She'd turned onto one of the roads off Las Olas, and

they both started looking at the house numbers to figure out which house they were going to.

"I think it's all the way at the end," she said. "That's where the biggest lots are. They were told we were coming?"

"Yes."

She'd been right about where the house was located. Once there, they were faced with a tall stucco wall with bougainvillea trailing over the top and an ornate metal gate. Pulling up close to a freestanding post with a speaker imbedded into it, Nychelle wound down her window and pressed the intercom button. When she told the man who answered who they were, the gate immediately began opening.

"Please follow the driveway to the right," the disembodied voice instructed. "Someone will meet you at the car park."

"Thank you," Nychelle called out, putting the car back into gear.

It was time to deal with their patient, but David resented the end of the trip. Despite Nychelle's initially cool attitude he'd enjoyed her company, as always, and they'd gotten back on a friendly footing. He didn't want that to fade away.

"By the way, your cousin Martin invited me to go out with him and his family next weekend."

Nychelle flicked him a sideways glance, then veered the car to the right, as instructed, and followed a brick-paved drive around the side of the huge Spanish-style house.

"They're lots of fun," she replied. "You should go."

Rounding the corner, she passed a fountain in the center of a wide paved area. Parking the car next to a high-end SUV, she turned off the ignition.

"Are you invited too?" he asked, trying to keep his voice light, although the tightness was back in his shoulders. "I mean, I hardly know Martin, so I figured he'd ask you to come along as well."

Swinging her legs out of the car, she replied, "Nope—and you'll be fine without me."

As he reached for his bag on the back seat David had to stop himself from arguing. And the fact he was supposed to be keeping his distance did nothing to alleviate his dissatisfaction when he thought about going without her.

CHAPTER NINE

CARMEN FITZPATRICK WAS as petite and pretty as she appeared on her album covers, but her *café au lait* skin was sallow, and a pair of wrinkles marred the spot between her eyebrows.

At first Nychelle thought the young woman was still in pain from her sickle cell crisis, but she soon realized at least part of her scowl was anger.

"I don't know what the fuss is all about," she said, as soon as David and Nychelle had been introduced. "Having you around is just a waste of time and money. I've been dealing with this since I was a child."

"Just stop your squawking." Milo LaMar, the man who'd met them outside and introduced himself as Carmen's manager, lowered himself onto one of the couches in the massive room and gave his artiste a glare. "You wanted to come down here, so we came. Making sure your health doesn't suffer because of the decision isn't a waste of anything."

Carmen snorted, matching his glower with a dagger stare from her dark, flashing eyes. "You're like an old woman, Milo. I'm fine."

They'd already received her medical records from the young doctor who'd flown in with her, and David had scanned them. Nychelle hung back slightly, letting him take the lead.

"Ms. Fitzpatrick, I'm glad you're feeling better, but your manager has a point." The young woman looked set to argue, but David smiled and held up his hand, forestalling her. "Most people recovering from a crisis wouldn't be traveling, much less going someplace where they don't already have a support system. We're here to make sure that whatever happens while you're in Florida will be dealt with as efficiently as it would be had you stayed in New York."

Carmen gave him a defiant look out of the corner of her eye. "I know what to do if a crisis comes on. I'm telling you—this isn't anything new to me."

"But living here is."

Nychelle liked the calm way David spoke: frankly, and not talking down to the patient.

Carmen gave a little head-toss. "I just need some peace and quiet. It's been a long few months. I just want to stay in one place for a while—preferably with no one coming by or wanting anything."

"Okay." David infused a little laughter into his voice. "We can take a hint, can't we, Nurse Cory? We'll get out of your hair as soon as we've given you a quick examination."

"We'll be gone in a flash," Nychelle agreed, handing David the medical bag. "Mr. LaMar, if you'd excuse us?"

Milo heaved his considerable bulk out of the sofa, then pointed a finger at Carmen. "Be nice. They're here to help you."

Carmen's rapid-fire spate of Spanish had Nychelle biting the inside of her lip to suppress slightly shocked laughter. The singer certainly knew how to get her point across in a colorful way, and Nychelle made sure not to look at David, in case his expression set her off.

Milo LaMar had warned them Carmen was feeling out of sorts—"Just not herself since this last crisis," was the way he'd put it—and Nychelle made sure to pay special attention to the younger woman's sullen mood.

When David started asking her about her condition, Carmen lost control.

"*Yes*, I've been taking my hydroxyurea. And, yes, it's been working fine." She was almost shouting, tears making her eyes gleam. "I *told* you—I've been dealing with this for most of my life. I don't need a pep talk or you going over everything all over again."

"So what's different this time?"

David's quiet question cut through her tirade and Carmen sank back into the corner of the couch, turning her head away.

"Nothing. Nothing's different. It's just the same life-interrupting garbage I've had to deal with all along."

"So why are you so upset this time?"

The silence stretched between them and Nychelle found herself holding her breath, almost afraid to move in case it stopped the young woman from opening up.

"Life was going so well." It was a whisper. "It had been almost two years since I had a crisis. The tour was great. I finally had someone I was interested in…"

Her voice faded, and Nychelle felt her heart contract in sympathy.

"He couldn't handle seeing you in the midst of the crisis?"

"It wasn't that… Oh, forget it. You wouldn't understand."

Nychelle took a chance, and sat down next to Carmen. "Maybe *I* would," she said quietly. "You didn't tell him about the sickle cell, did you?"

Carmen drew in a shuddering breath. "No. I don't tell anyone I don't think has to know. I never wanted anyone to say, *Oh, there's that Carmie-K—the chick with the sickle cell disease.* I never wanted to have people thinking about that instead of my music. Besides, we weren't really serious yet. Just getting to know each other."

"I get it," Nychelle said softly. "I really do."

Carmen whipped her head around to give her a glare. "How could you? You don't have it, do you?"

"No." Nychelle shook her head. "I don't. But I do have a condition I'd need any man I'm thinking of having a long-term serious relationship with to know about. The question becomes when do I tell him? It's not a first date conversation. Not even second or third. It's something I wouldn't want anyone I'm not planning a future with to know. So, then I have to figure out when's the best time? And sometimes it's easier to just forget about it."

"Yeah." Carmen nodded, tears trickling down her cheeks. "Yeah, exactly." She sighed. "I haven't had time for guys or relationships before, so it never came up. Then I was feeling so well that everything else other than the SCD just kind of became more important. I didn't have to think about it—like you said, just take my meds and go on with life. Then..."

Nychelle touched Carmen's hand—just a fleeting contact on the young woman's tightly fisted fingers. "Then the disease butted in, when it was least wanted?"

Finding the right words was difficult, but there was no way to sugarcoat the situation, and she doubted Carmen would appreciate it if she tried.

Drawing on her own experience, she said, "It's never going to be easy—but you know that already, and you have to live your life the way you want to. That includes what you keep private and what you share with others. It's tough for you, because you're in the public eye, and I really don't have any advice on how you should deal with that."

Carmen sighed, then said, "Yeah, it's gotten harder to keep it secret."

"At some point it will probably be in your best interests to go public with it." David shrugged slightly when Carmen threw him a scowl in response to his matter-of-fact statement. "I'm no expert on the press or social media, believe me, but it seems to me they thrive on ferreting out people's secrets and making a big deal out of them. If you choose to put the news out there, then it won't have the same impact."

"That's what Milo's been saying for the last year."

Slumped in the corner of the couch, Carmen looked forlorn. Funny how because of her talent and her poise Nychelle had forgotten just how young she really was.

"I just don't want the stares and the fuss—or to have it overshadow the music."

"It might for a while." David gave one of his abbreviated smiles. "But Nychelle advises me that you have many dedicated fans, and I'm sure they'll just want more music, no matter what."

"You know my music?"

Carmen's expression was skeptical, and Nychelle chuckled. "Yeah, yeah—I know I'm old..."

Carmen's stuttering, embarrassed reply just made her laugh harder, and soon David and then, after a few seconds, Carmen joined in.

By the time they left the mansion Carmen seemed in a better frame of mind. As Nychelle drove back toward the clinic David stretched his legs out as far as possible and said, "I think that went well." Looking at her, he continued, "We make a good team."

"Just about now I should probably tell you I've been trained to work smoothly with every doctor I come in contact with." Her lips quirked in a mischievous smile, and there was a twinkle of laughter in the glance she sent him. "But we both know it doesn't always work out that way."

David chuckled, even as his thumb beat an anxious tattoo on his thigh. "Yes, that's true. I'm just glad we seem to click. I think you did a great job finding out what was going on with Carmen."

Nychelle put on her indicator and checked her mirrors.

"You did too. So I guess you're right—we do make a pretty good team." She sighed. "I feel for her. It's hard having a disease that you know shortens your life expectancy as well as periodically completely disrupts your life."

"That's true—but sometimes you have to look at the positives too, right? Less than fifty years ago kids with sickle cell rarely lived past their early teens. That's not the case anymore."

"I know. I know… And the new bone marrow transplant treatment is promising. But not for her. She's an only child, and mixed race, so the chances of her finding a bone marrow match are miniscule."

He knew and admired many dedicated doctors and nurses, but Nychelle's seemingly unending well of knowledge and kindness was touching. Her remark about having a condition of her own had echoed in his head since she'd said it, and although it really was none of his business he had to ask.

Making his voice as casual as possible, he said, "You're a wonderful nurse, but I think your greatest asset is actually your empathy. Getting Carmen to talk by opening up about your own life is a good example of that." When Nychelle didn't say anything, he went on, "Were you telling the truth about having a medical condition?"

The car had stopped at a red light, but she didn't look at him when she replied, "Yes. I wouldn't make up something like that."

Her long, elegant fingers gripped the gearstick hard enough to make her knuckles pale. He should leave it alone. But, try as he might, he couldn't contain his fascination with the woman beside him, who haunted him even when she wasn't around. He kept telling himself to stay clear, yet he couldn't resist the need to know everything he could ferret out about her.

"So, what kind of condition is it?"

Nychelle pursed her lips slightly as she put the vehicle in gear and started to drive through the intersection. Then she relaxed, and shot him an impish glance. "Are you telling me you want a long-term intimate relationship with me?"

Okay.

The word leaped into his throat and literally froze him to his seat. How easy it would be to say it. And mean it.

Okay.

His temperature rose as fantasies of being with Nychelle wound through his head. He imagined silly things, like sharing the Sunday paper in bed, or laughing at a corny joke with her, and it made his heart rate go through the roof. Visualizing other, more important things sent an exciting, erotically charged ache spreading through his veins. Listening to her. Holding her. Making love to her.

Seeing her grow round with their baby

He clenched his teeth as fear shot like ice through his chest, banishing the arousing images. Then his heart clenched with a second jolt of terror.

Where had that thought come from? Why had it entered his head? Unless it was to remind him how dangerous it would be to get closer to Nychelle? He'd struggled these last few weeks, with memories of Natalie and the time after he'd lost her stronger than they'd been for a long time. Now guilt ate at him for even *thinking* such a thing.

David turned his head to stare, unseeing, out the side window, swallowing against the sour taste rising in his throat.

Nychelle snickered. "Ha! I didn't think so."

Suddenly tired, he battled competing emotions. Guilt and sorrow sat like molten iron in his belly, reminding him that he couldn't take another chance on love. He'd already had enough pain to last him a lifetime. There was no way he'd chance a repeat of the horrific agony he'd felt after losing Natalie. And yet his chest was tight with fear too.

Still looking out the window, unable to bear facing her, he asked, "Just tell me this then. Is it life-threatening? Your condition?"

"No," she replied, her tone subdued, as though his mood was affecting her. "No, nothing like that."

And for a moment, before he resolutely pulled himself together, relief made him literally weak. "Okay. Good. I'm glad to hear it."

CHAPTER TEN

NYCHELLE LEANED BACK in her office chair, her heart pounding a mile a minute, and pressed the cell phone tighter to her ear. She'd been as jumpy as a mouse at a cat convention all afternoon, waiting for a call from Dr. Miller's office. It had finally come, and now she was waiting for the doctor to pick up on her end. The canned instrumental music was no doubt meant to be soothing, but at that moment it was getting on her last nerve. Perhaps it was just as well the call had come now, when she'd been just about to leave the clinic. She was sure no matter what the news was there'd be tears involved.

These last few days she'd been on an emotional rollercoaster worse than any she'd ever experienced before. Normally she was good at compartmentalizing her life, keeping work, family and her personal business determinedly separate. That hadn't worked worth a damn these last forty-eight hours.

Tuesday morning she'd arrived at Lauderlakes and immediately looked for David's car in the staff parking lot. When she'd spotted the maroon Audi her heart had seemed about to jump straight out of her chest, and for the rest of the day she'd been on high alert.

It had been exhausting.

There was no good reason to be this het-up over him.

None at all. Surely it was her imagination that had her skin tingling every time she was around him?

The frequency of their encounters wasn't helping. From hardly being aware he existed, it seemed she couldn't avoid him, and now they were practically living in each other's pockets. Working together on Doug Comstock's case and then Carmen's, sitting on the planning committee for the next health fair—and, of course, going to the gala together.

Every time she thought about that night, and the kiss they'd shared, she shivered. Yet, there'd been no follow-up to that arousing encounter, so why couldn't she just forget it and move on?

David clearly had.

And she didn't want any follow-up, right? There was no place in her life for anything like that right now—*none.* Even if David was interested, which he obviously wasn't.

After she'd got home on Tuesday night she'd given herself another round of pep talks. She had really wished she could confide in Aliya, whom she knew would give her good advice. Unfortunately her cousin was also prone to saying, *I told you so*, and wouldn't hesitate to do so if Nychelle told her there was a man she was even slightly attracted to. That was the last thing Nychelle needed.

In fact, she'd thought, while putting together a salad she really hadn't wanted to eat, hearing those words at this particular time would no doubt make her burst into tears.

Nope. Didn't need it—any of it.

All she could realistically do was get over this attraction to David, because the alternative scenarios were too horrible to contemplate. If she continued to harbor these ridiculous longings they not only wouldn't be friends anymore, but even working with him would become impossible too. The problem was, she wasn't just in *lust* with him, she was…

Her mind had gone completely blank and she'd stared

down at the greens she'd just tossed with sunflower seeds, cucumber and red peppers.

You're what, exactly, Nychelle?

Her brain hadn't been inclined to come up with an answer, shying away and contemplating instead what dressing to put on the salad.

In her mind she'd heard her mother's voice say, *Avoidance*, and she'd snorted with irritation. Bad enough to be in this situation, but imagining her mom analyzing her too was ridiculous. Worse was knowing her diagnosis was probably correct. She was ducking thinking about her growing feelings for David, so as not to take the soul-searching to its logical, and no doubt painful, conclusion.

Sitting at the island, she looked around her home, suddenly lonely in a way she'd never been before within its walls. All the contentment she'd felt just a few short weeks ago seemed to have fled, leaving hollowness behind. Yet she couldn't allow herself to continue this way. She'd made a choice, and it was a good one. *That* was what she needed to remind herself whenever she started thinking about David. *The Plan* was in motion and she had to focus on staying healthy, both physically and emotionally. To do the latter she would just have to keep Dr. Heat discreetly at arm's length. Not rebuff him altogether. That would be too obvious. Just enjoy his friendship and nothing more.

Telling herself that a thousand times had finally had her convinced she was being stupid. It wasn't David causing her emotional upheaval at all. No. Surely these absurd mood swings, the icy dips and somersaults of her stomach, had nothing to do with him. Stressing about him was just a way to escape thinking about whether the IUI had worked. No doubt the uncomfortable physical reactions were actually about waiting for the next round of tests. After all, which was more important? There was no contest. Being pregnant trumped anything David could offer.

Right?

The excitement of knowing today was the day she would find out whether the IUI had been successful had buoyed her up all through Wednesday morning. That and her new determination had even allowed her to smile and wave at David in passing, although she hadn't stopped to talk.

The joy of anticipation had lasted up until her dash to Dr. Miller's office at lunchtime, and then quickly faded as she'd waited, none too patiently, to hear from the doctor. Now her stomach fluttered and rolled with nervous dread.

"Come on. Come *on*," she muttered, her hand aching from the strength of her grip on the cell phone.

As if hearing Nychelle's entreaty, the phone clicked and the music stopped, to be replaced by Dr. Miller's voice.

"Nychelle. Sorry to keep you waiting."

And just from the other woman's tone Nychelle knew what the OB/GYN would say next.

David paused at the corridor leading to Nychelle's office, wondering if she was still at work or had already left for the day.

He really wanted to see her.

Which annoyed the hell out of him.

Equally annoying was knowing there was no way to avoid this encounter. Carmen Fitzpatrick's test results were back and they needed to confer. With them both being tasked with her care, a case conference was inevitable.

He could have sent a message, asking her to come to his office, but he'd put it off all day and finally, when he hadn't been able to avoid it anymore, he'd accessed the staff schedule online to see if she might still be around. According to that, her last patient had been forty-five minutes ago. Hopefully she was finished with the appointment, but maybe was still writing up her notes.

Decision made, he strode down the corridor, refusing to

acknowledge the way his heart raced or the tension building at his nape. When he got to the waiting area outside of Nychelle's office he was glad to find just one medical assistant there, packing up her bag.

Lena looked up, and her eyebrows rose briefly in obvious surprise. "Dr. Warmington." She smiled, but it was a questioning smile rather than a friendly one. "What can I do for you?"

"Is Nurse Cory still around, Lena?" He held up the file in his hand.

The medical assistant's eyebrows dipped momentarily and she shot a quick glance at her watch as she replied, "She's still in her office, Doctor. Do you want me to ring through and ask if she's available?"

"That's okay."

At David's words Lena's hand fell back to her side, but not before she'd snuck another peek at her watch. Ah, yes. Lena was getting married in a few weeks. He remembered hearing her telling some of the nurses in the staff cafeteria.

Giving the woman a smile, he said, "You look like you have somewhere to be. Don't let me hold you up. I'll just knock and see if she has time to talk to me."

Lena grinned, her face lighting up as she grabbed her bag. "Thank you, Doctor. Have a good evening."

David watched her walk away, then stepped over to Nychelle's door. Hand poised to knock, he paused and took a deep breath, his heart rate going into overdrive. His reaction to her infuriated him, made him determined to, once and for all, get past it.

They were colleagues—nothing else.

They would never be anything else. He wouldn't let them be.

With another deep breath, he rapped on the door and then, responding to the muffled reply from inside, unlatched it and pushed it open.

Nychelle was looking out of the window when David stepped through the door, and something about her posture arrested his forward momentum. She was so still she hardly seemed to be breathing and, judging from her reflection in the glass, her usually expressive face was blank. The heat of his resolve bled away, was replaced by a cold spike of surprise.

"Nychelle?" He said her name softly as he stepped completely into the room and closed the door behind him.

She turned to look at him, but the movement was stiff and her eyes were blank, slightly glazed, as though with shock. Did she even know he was there?

It only took a couple of strides to get to her side, to reach out and touch her face. Warmth bloomed beneath his fingers as she leaned her cheek into his palm and closed her eyes. Her face relaxed, and the slight tilt of her lips was beatific. She'd never looked more beautiful, and David's heart stuttered.

He'd come into her office wanting to get her off his mind, to get over the crazy attraction he'd felt. Seeing her like that, leaning so trustingly into his hand, he realized it would probably never happen. If anything, his feelings would only deepen.

But giving in to them would lead him back down a path he refused to traverse again. Down that road lay the giving of his heart to another, risking the devastation he'd lived through once before and couldn't imagine surviving again.

The coldness in his belly flooded through him, invading his limbs, making his chest tighten almost sickeningly. Yet although he wanted to step back, he forced himself to stay where he was, concern for Nychelle somehow still foremost in his mind.

Swallowing, he found the wherewithal to ask, "Nychelle, are you okay? What's happened?"

Her eyelids fluttered and then opened. The glow in her

eyes made his heart contract again, but she just shook her head and stepped back. Disappointment making him frown, David let his hand fall back to his side, instead of using it to pull her close the way he wanted to.

"Don't shake your head at me." It was little better than a growl, but he couldn't stop the way annoyance had tightened his throat. "There's something going on. Tell me."

Her eyes widened momentarily, her eyebrows rising, no doubt at his demanding tone. Yet her voice was soft and calm when she replied, "I just got some good news." She lifted her hand, as though to forestall whatever he might say next. "I'm not going to share it. Sorry."

It wasn't his place to demand that she tell him, and he had no reason to believe she would feel inclined to tell him even if he did demand it, but he had to swallow again so as not to do exactly that. He scowled at her, torn, and for some reason that made her laugh.

"Thank you," she said, stepping back, still smiling.

"For what?"

She gave a little shrug. "For being here at this exact moment."

Confused, he shook his head. "Share your news and I'll celebrate with you."

With a chuckle she shook her head again, taking another step back as she did so. "I can't. But I'm happy you were the one I almost spilled the beans to."

The radiance of her face, the memories of the trusting way she'd leaned on him and the softness of her smile overcame all his defenses. Something inside him gave way, collapsed, and then was incinerated in a wave of desire so intense it was irresistible.

With a groan of surrender he stepped forward and drew her unresisting form into his embrace. Looking into her stunning eyes, he tried to pull himself back from the brink, but couldn't get his arms to release her, couldn't back away.

All good intentions fled as yearning for her overwhelmed him completely.

CHAPTER ELEVEN

SHE'D SEEN HIS eyes serious, and seen them smiling. Nychelle even thought she'd seen them hot with passion. But now she knew what she'd experienced the night of the gala had been little more than warmth, since now they blazed.

The joy and gratitude she'd felt on learning the IUI had been successful still swam in her veins, but now it was joined by a new kind of elation. One that sparked and zinged through every synapse, brought on by being held in David's arms.

An almost preternatural stillness fell; Nychelle couldn't move, couldn't breathe, and David seemed similarly afflicted. His face was frozen into an expression of such tender ferocity it caused tears to prickle the backs of her eyes. She'd never suspected how beautiful being looked at like that would make her feel, or how it would make her already powerful arousal spike to incendiary levels.

Which one of them moved first was an immaterial question, lost in the wonder of David's lips on hers, the passion of their kiss. He aligned their bodies so she fit snugly between his legs, and when his arms tightened around her Nychelle melted into him, bones and muscles going liquid with desire and pleasure.

From the hard length of his erection pressing against her

stomach there could be no doubt as to how much he wanted her. It was also in the tangle of their tongues, the way they devoured each other's mouths.

His strong hands slid down her back to grip her bottom and pull her even closer. The heat radiating from their bodies was a physical manifestation of the need flowing like lava between them. The want.

There was no hesitation in their embrace. The way he held her was masterful, compelling, and she loved it. She'd never felt delicate or treasured in a man's arms before, but somehow in David's she did.

A sound of passion broke from his throat, and the ache that had been building in her nipples, between her legs, intensified and became almost unbearable. And when his mouth left hers to slide down to her throat she gasped, echoing his delight. Finding the hem of her tunic top, he slid his hands beneath to find the bare skin of her back, causing her to arch, to rub against him, wanton under the spell of his lovemaking.

"Nychelle..."

It was a growl against her neck, causing a delicious shiver to climb her spine and bringing a little spasm of pleasure.

"So beautiful. So sexy."

She'd have said the same about him, but words deserted her as his lips kissed and sucked with glorious effect along her skin. When his hands slid to her sides, his thumbs lightly caressing the curves of her breasts, she was already trembling, longing for even deeper contact. His mouth moved lower, to the sensitive curve where neck met shoulder, and she whispered a plea, arching to offer him her breasts, almost sobbing with relief when his palm brushed one nipple through her bra.

Strong, tender fingers closed around her breast, caressing it, and his thumb rubbed back and forth across the straining peak. She worked at pulling his shirt from his pants then opening it, wanting skin-to-skin contact. He followed her lead, unbuttoning her tunic and pushing the edges aside. When he undid the front closure of her bra it crossed her mind that she'd never felt this aroused, especially this quickly, but the thought was lost in a burst of ecstasy when his lips closed around one oversensitized nipple. The draw of his mouth and the damp sweep of his tongue had her crying out softly, the pleasure almost too much to bear.

"David!"

"Yes," he replied, causing cool air to rush over her flesh, bringing another, stronger tremor between her legs.

Had she ever been this close to orgasm without a touch there? She didn't think so. The craving grew, had her pressing against him, ready and willing for whatever came next, wanting more and more.

He knew. How could he not know when she was being so blatant? Somehow one of his legs had made its way between hers and she rocked against it, getting closer and closer to coming with each undulation of her hips.

"God..." It was a groan against her skin, and the vibrations traveled from his lips into her, driving her higher. "I have to—"

David picked her up as though she weighed nothing at all. With a few long strides they were at the desk, and when he lowered her to sit on it Nychelle wrapped her legs around his waist.

The opening notes of a nineties rap song reverberated through the room, the sound so jarring they both jumped.

They froze as the cellphone ring tone stopped for an instant. When it started again David stepped back so quickly Nychelle rocked in place, almost sliding from the desk. Their gazes collided, and in his expression Nychelle read the same shock she knew was mirrored on her face.

Tugging her tunic closed with one hand, she reached unthinkingly for the phone with the other. When David turned away and began buttoning his shirt she went cold with remorse—and something deeper. Sadder. The ringing phone had broken a beautiful erotic spell. One that should never have been cast.

Taking a shuddering inhalation, she looked away, so he wouldn't see the threatening tears.

"Hey, Nychelle, what's going on?"

Martin's voice made her realize she'd actually answered the phone, but it took her a moment to gather herself and reply. "N…nothing much."

"Is this a bad time? You sound like you're busy."

Probably because she was holding the phone between her shoulder and chin while fumbling to refasten her bra. "No, it's fine. What's up?"

"I just texted David Warmington, reminding him about my invitation to go out with the family this coming weekend, and I want you to come too. After all, he and I only met briefly once, before the gala. It'll be good for him to have someone there he knows a little better."

Hearing his name made her automatically look toward David. Luckily he still had his back to her, but watching him straighten his clothing made her icy veins heat through.

She quickly looked away. "I… I don't think…"

"Aw, come on, cuz." Martin was using his wheedling voice—the one he knew she found hard to resist. "We've hardly seen you over the last few months. Leighann and MJ keep asking when you'll be by."

"Let me get back to you on that, okay?"

She'd finally got her tunic buttoned, but felt as if her bra was crooked. Even being fully dressed didn't mitigate her deep discomfort. What the heck were they thinking, making out like teenagers on her desk? What the heck was *she* thinking, especially after the news she'd just received about her pregnancy?

"I have some things I have to take care of before I can make a decision."

Things like making sure David Warmington agreed that what had just happened had been a huge mistake and wouldn't happen again.

No matter how much she wished it would.

His insides swirling with a mixture of arousal, surprise and self-recrimination, David moved over to the window in Nychelle's office and stood looking out, trying to ignore the soft murmur of her voice.

He wanted to leave—just take off without saying anything—but that would be the coward's way out. Nychelle deserved better.

And that was the whole truth of it. Nychelle deserved the very best life had to offer—everything a man had to give—and he didn't have everything to give anymore. There was an important part of his heart and soul that was dead, killed by grief and fear. Or at the very least was locked away where no one could ever reach. Not even someone as amazing as Nychelle.

And there was no way to explain that without exposing his pain, ripping away the thin scab over his wounds. As much as he wanted to crush whatever it was building between them once and for all, he wanted her sympathy even less. No. Best to simply pretend, once more, that it didn't matter, and then make himself believe it didn't.

But, either way, he had to put a stop to this…this…

His brain stumbled, unable or unwilling to find the appropriate word for the emotions and impulses that overcame him whenever Nychelle was near. All he knew was that they had to stop.

The room was silent, and he realized she must have finished her call and hung up. He made his expression as stoic as he could, then turned to face her. Before he could speak she held up her hands, as though ready to push anything he said back at him.

"Don't." She shook her head, her lips wavering into something that he figured was supposed to be a smile. "There's no need to say it."

Perversely, now it appeared she was thinking along the same lines as he was, he had the sudden urge not to just let it go.

"Say what?"

"That what just happened was a mistake. Believe me, I agree wholeheartedly." She straightened, taking on an air of dignity and resolve. "I'm not in the habit of leading men on. I'm also not in the habit of having casual sex." She shrugged slightly before she added, "And that's all I could offer you—sex that, even casual, could have unwanted repercussions for us both."

He wasn't sure what "repercussions" she was worried about for herself, but knew what he needed to avoid. It would be so easy to fall for Nychelle, to begin craving her love…

Spinning on his heel, he bent down to retrieve the folder, which he'd dropped in his eagerness to get closer to Nychelle. He really needed to get away—to think about what had happened. Being around Nychelle twisted his emotions into crazy knots and he needed to unravel them, to figure out exactly what to do. Yet it felt wrong. As though there was more that should be said.

Before he could figure it out she slid off the desk and glanced down at the file in his hand. "So, did you want to talk to me about a patient?"

Just like that the sensation of sharing something special vanished, leaving him strangely flat. When she circled her desk, staying as far away as possible, the small act of avoidance made his chest ache.

"Yes." He opened the file, gathering his composure. "Carmen's tests are back."

"Anything unusual?"

"Her iron levels are elevated. Not unusual in someone who just underwent a transfusion, but something I'd suggest we keep an eye on."

Nychelle sat in her chair and pulled it close to the desk, as though to put a physical barrier between them. "If you leave the results with me, I'll forward them to the hematologist and make sure our notes are up to date."

She was rubbing her right wrist, and he took an impulsive step forward. "Are you hurt? Did I hurt you?" Just the thought made him angry.

"What? No. Why do you ask?"

"You're rubbing your wrist." He remembered seeing her do it before, but this time it worried him. Reaching the desk, he held out his hand to her. "Let me see."

Immediately she stopped, dropping her hands to her lap. "It's fine, David."

The snappish reply brought him up short. He wasn't used to that from her.

"It's just a nervous habit from when I was a child. I broke my wrist one summer, and got used to rubbing it after the cast came off, when it ached. Nothing to worry about."

Somehow hearing her admit to her own disquiet made his dissipate slightly, and he nodded. "Fair enough."

Their eyes met, and the confusion in her gaze made that stupid ache in his chest expand. He wanted to comfort her, even as he acknowledged that it was the worst thing he could possibly do.

She looked away, down at the file in his hand, and nodded toward the desk. "Leave it with me and I'll deal with it."

"Thank you." He set the file on her desk and without

another word made his feet take him toward the door, even though they were inclined to stay exactly where they were.

"David?"

The soft sound of his name on her lips froze him in place, his hand grasping the door handle but not unlatching it. He didn't turn, fearing looking at her, and felt the desire still thrumming through his veins despite it all. "Yes?"

"That was Martin on the phone. He's invited me to come along this weekend."

"I haven't had a chance to say yes or no myself," he replied. His knuckles were turning white from his tight grip on the handle. "If you don't want to go, or don't want *me* to go—"

"No, it's not that. It's just..."

"You want to make sure it won't be awkward?" Risking a glance back at her, he forced a small smile. "I can handle it. Can you?"

"Yes. Of course." She neither looked nor sounded convinced. "It'll be...fun."

"Okay." He opened the door and lifted his hand in farewell, eager to leave before he gave in to the impulse to ask her what she'd *really* wanted to say. "See you then, if not before."

But he hoped it wasn't before. He wanted as much time as possible to exorcize his growing need and the agonizing desire he felt for Nychelle. Time to figure out how he could keep her friendship without losing his heart in the process.

CHAPTER TWELVE

"PINK EYE?" NYCHELLE plopped down onto her kitchen stool. "MJ has pink eye?"

"Can you dig it?" Martin sounded harassed and annoyed. "Woke up with it this morning—on the first day of summer vacation, to boot."

"Oh, no. What about Leighann?"

"So far, so good, and we're doing everything we can to stop her from contracting it. Jennifer's been running around with antiseptic wipes all morning. Martin Tremaine Girvan Junior!" Martin suddenly shouted, the bellow only slightly muffled by what Nychelle suspected was him pointing the phone at his son. "Do. Not. Scratch. Your. Eye. Mom will be back in a minute with some drops to make it stop itching."

Nychelle chuckled, suppressing it when he said, "He's driving us crazy—alternately whining, rubbing his eye, and threatening to infect his sister. We're supposed to be going on vacation in ten days, but if Leighann gets it we may have to cancel."

"Hopefully that won't happen."

"From your lips to God's ear," Martin grumbled. "Just coordinating a vacation with our schedules is hard enough. And, speaking of canceling, I was planning to take you and David out on the boat today, but I can't risk taking MJ anywhere. Not fair to leave Jen here to suffer by herself either."

Nychelle stared out the window, biting her lip as a combination of disappointment and relief swirled through her. "Well, it can't be helped. Taking care of your family is the most important thing. We'll go out another time."

"I don't want to disappoint David."

There were a few more moments of muffled shouting, and Nychelle figured the phone was clasped to her cousin's chest this time, so she wouldn't hear the threats he was making to his son.

"Sorry about that. This boy is a menace."

"He's eight. What do you expect? At that age you were a pain too."

"I was not."

Nychelle chuckled at his lofty tone.

"I was a perfect little paragon. All right. All *right*." He interrupted her laughter to get back to what he was saying. "We can't go out on the boat, but I went ahead and bought two tickets for you guys to take the river taxi. It'll be a good way for you to show David more of the city without having to think about parking."

"I'm sure he won't mind if you have to cancel—"

"I already talked to him and told him you were willing to go."

"What? Without talking to me first?"

Martin obviously wasn't listening to her. If he had been he surely would have heard the outrage in her voice and put even a hint of remorse into his reply. Instead, he just said, "I knew you wouldn't mind. I'll email you the tickets, and he'll come to pick you up at ten."

Nychelle clenched her teeth to hold back her instinctive refusal. Would she never get away from this man? Well, maybe that was too harsh. David was the one man she both craved and was afraid to be around. How many times had she decided it would be best to avoid him, only to end up in his presence almost immediately thereafter?

"It'll be fun." Ironic to have Martin quoting her own words back at her. "He seems like a nice guy. Don't you think so?"

"Yes, he's a nice guy." Resigned to her fate, she sighed. "It's fine. Take care of the family."

"Awesome. Thanks, Nych. Call me later and let me know how it goes."

"Okay. Will do."

Almost before she'd finished speaking Martin was hollering at MJ again as he hung up.

Putting the phone down on the counter, Nychelle rubbed her suddenly aching temple.

Two days before, she'd finally given in to the need to speak to someone about David and told Aliya what had happened between them.

"The timing isn't optimal," her cousin had said. "But I guess the real question is, what do you want to do about it?"

"I don't know," Nychelle had confessed, tears welling. "I'm confused."

For two people who claimed to want to be friends, David and she constantly seemed willing—no, determined to put strain on their relationship. Making out like teenagers. Blowing hot and cold. Hiding from each other instead of coming clean.

Well, okay, that last one was all her. And, while she'd agreed that it would be wise for them both to forget what had happened in her office, she found herself thinking and dreaming about making love with David all the time. Then getting angry with herself.

Since meeting him she'd been a mass of contradictions and seesawing emotions.

Which was why she knew she had to stop seeing him.

"You have feelings for him." Aliya hadn't asked, simply stated it as a fact. "I know you, and you wouldn't have been making out with him if you didn't."

"I—" She'd wanted to disagree, but the lie wouldn't pass her lips. Instead she'd concentrated on not sniffling, hoping Aliya wouldn't realize she was crying.

"Don't tell me you don't. I won't believe you." Then her cousin's voice had softened. "Listen, best-case scenario is he has feelings for you too, and won't care that you're pregnant. Worst-case is that he does care, and his feelings aren't strong enough for him to see past it. But the only way you're going to know what will happen…"

"Is for me to tell him." Abandoning her attempt to hide her tears from her cousin, Nychelle had blown her nose. "I know I should—but it's all happened so suddenly. It feels as though I'm making more out of the situation than I should."

"Have the conversation, Nych. Whichever way it goes, at least you'll know."

Aliya was right, of course.

Now restless, Nychelle got up and wandered over to the sliding glass door. Looking out at the verdant greenery in her backyard usually calmed her, but today it didn't. In less than half an hour she'd be thrown into David's company again. Just thinking about it made her body tighten and heat. No other man had ever had this effect on her—not even Nick, who she'd thought was her forever guy. Despite telling herself it was hormones, deep down she knew it wasn't. This attraction was too intense, too multifaceted to dismiss.

If it had just been the physical attraction, she probably could have ignored it, but what she couldn't disregard was how deeply she liked and admired him too. Long gone were her fears about his character. Everything she'd seen about him told her he was trustworthy, and a genuinely wonderful man. It wouldn't take much to push her over into falling for him completely.

So, yes, she was going to have to deal with it…

But not today.

This chance to spend time with him was, in a way, a gift. She was going to take advantage of the opportunity to simply take pleasure in his company without strings or overanalyzing.

It'll be a last hurrah.

The decision was calming, soothing, giving her permission to enjoy the day without giving too much weight to what would happen next.

Buoyed by that thought, she went to finish getting ready, excitement tingling over her skin.

David glanced over at Nychelle as he steered the car into the river cruise parking structure. She looked relaxed, and that made his trepidation wane.

Bearing in mind their encounter in her office, he hadn't known what to expect, and when Martin had explained the situation his first impulse had been to suggest they postpone their outing until the whole family could go. But Martin had insisted Nychelle was expecting him, and David hadn't wanted to sound churlish, or make a big deal out of it when she obviously didn't care.

There had been a hint of tension in the air, but after a slightly stiff greeting at her door it had mostly dissipated.

"The riverfront area is nice to walk through. Good restaurants and shopping, if you're into that kind of thing."

She'd been acting like a tour guide, pointing out various places of interest, like the Broward Center for the Performing Arts and the Museum of Discovery and Science, along with a Jamaican restaurant she said was amazing.

While he parked in an empty space she continued, "I prefer to go there when it's a little cooler. Somehow the heat isn't as bad when you're on the water."

She didn't wait for him to open her door, but got out immediately and, closing the door with a firm snap, gestured toward the exit.

"Let's go find us a water taxi."

When he rounded the back of the car she'd started walking, but then suddenly she stopped and turned to face him.

"Listen," she said. "I know we should talk about what happened between us. It's the adult thing to do. But can we shelve it for now and just enjoy the day?" Her hands fluttered between them. "I just need some more time to get things straight in my head, okay?"

He should be thankful—and a part of him was. Rubbing the back of his neck, he once more contemplated just how confused and contradictory his feelings were when it came to her. Even though he'd repeatedly told himself the best thing they could do was pretend none of it had happened and maintain the status quo, the urge to push, to find out exactly what she was thinking, was strong.

Yet this was an opportunity to simply be with her, without worrying about what his emotions meant or what to do about them. So, accepting her request to put it all aside for the day, he nodded. "Okay. So where do we go from here?"

Nychelle looked around, choosing to ignore the less literal interpretation of his words.

"This way," she said, pointing down a pathway.

"Do we need to buy tickets?" David asked as they approached the riverside restaurant where apparently they'd board the taxi.

"No, Martin got them online and I printed the vouchers. I thought about booking one of the guided tours," she told him, leading him into the restaurant. "But this way we can get off and on the taxis whenever we want, without being tied down to a specific route."

"Wow, this place is…colorful." David looked at the ceiling, where all manner of nautical gear and beach-themed tchotchkes hung.

A large wooden mermaid caught his attention. When

he raised his eyebrows at her suggestive pose, Nychelle giggled.

"It's a true tourist spot," she told him, petting a plastic parrot with an eye patch and still chuckling. "But although some these things are just kitsch, many things are real equipment used on boats in the past."

David smiled at that, his mood lightening even more with her laughter. "You don't have to tell me." Pointing at his chest, he went on, "South Carolinian, remember? I recognize the glass fishing globes and old-school breathing apparatus."

"Darn it." She added a pout to her disgruntled tone. "You're spoiling my tour guide spiel!"

"Okay, I won't say another word."

David mimed zipping and locking his lips, then throwing away the key. It was silly, and not something he'd usually do unless he was around his family, who knew and understood his lighter side, but it felt natural to show this aspect of himself to Nychelle.

"You nut."

Nychelle swatted him on the arm, and he hoped their easy camaraderie would last for the whole day. It felt so right.

"Do you want a drink before the taxi comes?" she asked.

"Mmph-mmm-hmm-mmm." Keeping his lips pressed together was hard, with a grin trying its best to break through, and when Nychelle swatted him again David couldn't hold back his laughter. "Hey, I promised not to say another word."

"Oh, you…*you…*"

"Careful, Nurse Cory." He gave her a stern look, knowing his twitching lips gave away his amusement. "Let's not sully that sweet, professional disposition everyone talks about."

"Ha!" Turning up her nose, she replied, "At least no one at work calls me names like *Dr. Heat*."

"Argh!" He was still smiling, but embarrassment made warmth spread across his face. "One of the other doctors told me about that and I thought he was kidding."

"Nope." She was giggling so hard she could barely get the word out, and she took a couple of hitched breaths before she continued. "In the nurses' lounge it's all, 'Dr. Heat said this…' and 'Dr. Heat is so dreamy…' It's a wonder your ears don't burn all day long."

"Now you're just being a brat." He lifted her hand and nipped the knuckle of her index finger. "Stop that."

"Ow." She pouted again, and tried to pull away. "Just because you don't appreciate being sexualized it doesn't mean you can be nasty when it's pointed out."

"'Sexualized?'" He groaned dramatically. "That's what I get for going out with a psychiatrist's daughter? Big words and overanalyzing?"

She opened her mouth, as though to make a scathing rebuttal, but instead broke out in giggles again.

David couldn't maintain his air of indignation either, and soon cracked under the strain of their combined silliness—so much so that when the water taxi drew up to the dock they practically reeled toward it, rather than walked.

The crew member who checked their vouchers grinned at them. "You folks look like you're already enjoying the day."

"It's a gorgeous one," Nychelle replied, and David nodded his agreement.

Watching her face, her brilliant smile, had him thinking the perfect, cloudless day was nowhere near as beautiful as she was.

They made their way to one of the seats in the shade, near the bow, and he settled onto the padded bench beside her, appreciating the breeze coming off the water. Around them the boat filled up, a cacophony of diverse languages filling the air as different groups came aboard.

"Do many locals use the river taxis?" he asked.

"Not really," Nychelle replied. "It's more of a tourist thing—although bar-hopping along the waterfront using the taxis as transportation can be fun. It's easier than trying to find parking if you want to go to the beach too." She chuckled and shook her head. "But most people are so used to driving they don't remember it's available."

David tipped his head back to catch more of the breeze. "The tourists have it right. I'd rather do this than drive in circles looking for a parking space."

"Me too." Nychelle was still smiling. "There's always a little wind to stir the air when you're on the water, so it really is a nice way to travel. Far nicer than being in an air-conditioned car."

"Ha!" He snorted. "Don't knock the air-conditioning. I've really come to love Florida, but the heat and humidity takes some getting used to."

"I'm sure it does," she replied. "Especially after being in Chicago."

As they chatted about the hazards of winter, and how different it was in the south, the boat pulled away from the dock and the captain set a leisurely course down the New River.

"Have you convinced your parents to come visit yet?" Nychelle turned sideways on the seat, so she was facing him to ask the question.

"Not yet." He gazed toward the north shore, his amusement waning. "I've got my sister working on them too." Thinking about his no-nonsense little sister made him smile again. "Of course, Mary-Liz says if they won't come she and the kids would be happy to take their place."

"Of course!" Nychelle chuckled, shifting to put her arm

up on the bench cushion behind her. "Why don't your parents want to come?"

Again, not something he'd usually discuss, but talking to her was so easy. "They haven't traveled much, and just thinking about navigating through airports makes my mom break out in hives." She nodded, and he liked it that she showed no amusement about their fears. He continued, "Dad would never admit that's the case with him too, but he doesn't have to. I know the truth."

Glancing down at the hand lying casually in her lap, he wished he had the right to take it and hold it. Instead he looked out over the water again.

"He has heart problems, and I'm a little worried the strain may bring on an angina attack, so I'm not pushing too hard."

As though reading his mind, Nychelle gave his hand a quick squeeze. When she let go, he immediately missed the contact.

"Have you thought about going up and then having them fly back with you? Or, if they really don't want to fly, driving them down? It's about nine hours from Atlanta to here. How long a drive would it be from where they live?"

Emotion rushed warm and sweet through his chest and he couldn't help staring at her as he replied, "About the same."

Nychelle lifted a hand to smooth her hair, the gesture uncertain. "Why are you looking at me that way?"

"Why didn't *I* think of that?" He shook his head. Then, throwing caution to the wind, he reached out to thread his fingers through hers, and was ridiculously happy when she didn't tug her hand away. "You're incredible."

"Don't be silly." She dipped her head, as though shy, and the warmth in his chest spread out into his belly. "You would have thought of it sooner or later."

"Probably not," he replied, tightening his grip on her

hand when she gently tried to pull it free. She stilled. "It's the kind of solution only someone with a completely empathetic soul would come up with straight off the bat."

She looked at him and said quickly, "By the way, keep an eye out for manatees. They're the reason the boat has to go so slowly, and every now and then you'll see a tail pop up out of the water."

"Okay," he replied, but his gaze never left her face and he felt no inclination to look away.

CHAPTER THIRTEEN

DAVID KEPT STARING, and Nychelle was the one who looked away first. It felt as though something important had just happened, yet she didn't know what. Rushing to speak, she tried for a much less intimate subject, hoping to curtail the tension flowing between them.

"By the way, while I remember, our patient Carmen Fitzpatrick released a statement to the media about having sickle cell disease."

"Really?" There was genuine surprise in his voice, and when she looked at him his eyebrows were raised. "I thought she was fanatical about her privacy?"

"She always has been, but maybe she decided it was better to do it when she wanted to, rather than have someone dig it up and blindside her—like you and her manager said might happen."

"Hmm." Leaning back, still staring intently at her, he asked, "How did you find out?"

"Martin's daughter, Leighann, told me. Once the news broke she looked up the disease and had questions." Nychelle shook her head. "Her parents are both doctors but she called me for information and to discuss it. Go figure."

"She probably knows you'll give it to her straight. Besides, you're both fans, so it makes sense to talk to you about it rather than her parents."

"I guess..."

She feigned interest in the passing scenery and pushed her sunglasses farther up her nose, still a little shaken by the strangely intimate moment they'd just shared. This man could upset her equilibrium like no one ever had before. The way he watched her, whether smiling or, like just now, with that serious, searching expression, just made her shiver.

Lost in thought, she was a little surprised when he reverted to their previous conversation.

"So, how do you know how long it takes to drive to Atlanta? Do you go there often?"

"A few times a year, usually, since my cousin Aliya—Martin's little sister—moved there four years ago. I don't always drive, but sometimes I just like the idea of a road trip."

"You're close?"

"Best friends practically since we were born." She smiled at the thought of Aliya and her craziness, and her excitement at the thought of being an honorary auntie. "We spent all our time at each other's houses...went to school together. Our families even migrated at the same time, so it was only when we went to college that we were first really apart."

"Don't tell me—she's a doctor too?"

Nychelle nodded. "Uh-huh. An hematologist-oncologist, specializing in research into childhood hematological cancers and the effect of known cancer treatments on kids."

David's lips quirked. "You really *do* come from a family of overachievers, don't you?"

Nychelle gave him a grin. "You know it."

The boat had already stopped a couple of times to pick up passengers and was now once more edging toward shore.

"Ooh," she said, pointing, hoping to distract him. "That's the Stranahan House Museum. It's reputed to be haunted and they sometimes have ghost tours, including a night-time boat ride."

David seemed less interested in the historic house than he was in her life, though.

"Why was it that you decided not to become a doctor too? It seems as though it's a family tradition."

She hesitated, torn between complete honesty and a slightly less revealing version of the truth. Today wasn't the day to get too deep, she reminded herself.

Just keep it light.

"Overachieving requires a singularity of focus I've never truly been interested in. I wanted to have a life outside of work. Have room for days like today, when there's nothing more pressing than drifting down a river, having a laugh or two."

He leaned back against the cushions and even with his dark glasses in place she knew he was subjecting her to another of his intent stares. It caused little prickles of awareness to tiptoe along her spine.

"But I'm a doctor, and I'm here drifting down the river too."

"Sure." She nodded. "But how old were you when you finished your residency?"

"Thirty," he replied.

"There you go." She waved a hand for emphasis. "I'm not quite thirty yet, and I've been out of school and living my life for a while—whereas I'm sure you've had to put off a lot of stuff, make a lot of sacrifices, to get to where you are now. I've been able to do some traveling, save up for a house and advance my career, all within the frame of time it took you to graduate. That's what I wanted, rather than MD after my name. Aliya is brilliant—she graduated far earlier than her peers and has already made a name for herself—but she admits she wishes she'd had more of a life when she was in college."

There was much more to it, but she hoped he wouldn't dig any deeper.

Trying to steer him off that track, she continued, "And you yourself said my job is just as important as yours. Did you mean it, or were you just trying to annoy my father?"

"Not at all." David paused as the boat bumped the dock near Stranahan House, putting one large, warm hand on her arm as if to steady her. "I *do* believe it." He grinned. "Besides, if I really wanted to aggravate your dad I'd have said your job was more important than mine—and his."

She laughed at the thought of her father's face if David had said that to him, and turned to watch as more passengers boarded the boat. There was a family of seven: parents, another couple who looked to be grandparents, and three children—the oldest no more than eight or so, the youngest just a baby in the mother's arms. They all looked happy except for the baby, who appeared to be sleeping, and a pang of longing so strong it made her breath catch swept through Nychelle.

That was what she wanted. *That* was why she'd forgone the rigors of medical school for what her parents had called "a wasted opportunity." Of course they would never understand. The concept of not wanting to be called *Doctor*, of believing there was more to life than work, was alien to them both.

The water taxi rocked as more people climbed on, and as though reacting to the motion the baby awoke, squirming, her face scrunched up in objection. Nychelle couldn't help smiling, thinking about the life growing in her belly, and longing for the day she would be holding her own baby.

Nychelle was so focused on whatever it was she was looking at that David's gaze followed hers to where a young woman sat, holding a squirming baby. In deference to the heat the baby was uncovered except for a pink and yellow onesie and a pair of rather snazzy striped socks. Her face was red with temper, her hair plastered down on one side and wildly curly on the other.

David instinctively looked away, as he always did when seeing a baby outside of a work setting. Yet, he found his gaze drawn back.

It was only then he realized that the hard pang of grief he used to feel whenever he saw a baby was absent.

When had that happened?

Now he waited for guilt to take its place—was shocked when there was no hint of that emotion either. Was he the same man who, on the anniversary of Natalie's birth, suffered all the agony of losing a child as if it had just happened?

But that wasn't quite right, either. He remembered what it had been like when it had happened. The agonizing, almost paralyzing sense of loss. The inability to think about anything other than Natalie. The urgent need to somehow turn back the clock and save her, even though logically he knew it was impossible.

He'd mourned on her last birthday, and still thought of her often, but not to the exclusion of all else. Not in the way he had at first, and for a long time after, when it had been a Herculean effort to see past the pain so as to go on with his life. A little at a time he'd learned to live with the knowledge that she was gone and was never coming back.

"Look, Mom. *Look!*"

A child's excited shriek gave him a good reason to look away from the baby, to pretend interest in where the little girl was pointing, out into the river. Still lost in his ruminations, David hardly saw the ripples in the water, barely registered the flip of a large, dark tail and the lively chatter the brief appearance of the manatee had caused.

"Did you see it?"

"I did." He nodded, wondering if she meant the manatee or the baby, since she'd been as intent on the latter as he.

"The first one you've seen since you came here?"

"Yes, although I still don't think I've seen one properly," he replied, aware of a dual meaning to his words that she wouldn't understand, and gaining a chuckle from her.

"True. A tail does not a manatee make, right?" When he laughingly agreed, she said, "I've always wanted to go to the Three Sisters Springs, on the west coast, and see them where they winter. Apparently you can get a really good look at them there."

"Why haven't you?"

She lifted a hand to push her sunglasses firmly up on her nose. "My ex-fiancé didn't like the outdoors much—preferred to holiday at casinos and resorts. Although it's been a while since we broke up, I just haven't made the trip."

The news that she'd been engaged gave him a jolt, and it struck him then how little they really knew about each other. Their friendship had grown in fits and starts, without any of the revelations that would naturally have emerged had they been dating. He'd told her very little about himself too, so it wasn't one-sided.

They'd agreed to keep things light between them today, but he didn't think that meant they were barred from talking about themselves.

"You should go," he said, leaning back and putting his arm along the cushion behind her, so the end of her ponytail brushed his hand. "When my marriage broke up I went white-water rafting. My ex refused to even consider it when we were together, and it was something I'd dreamt of doing since I was a child."

"I thought I'd heard you'd been married but I didn't want to bring it up, in case it was too painful."

She was in profile to him, and he saw her eyes flick toward him behind her dark glasses. The sideways glance was accompanied by that habitual rubbing of her wrist, and it made him want to stroke her nape with a calming finger.

"It was a while ago, so not painful anymore."

The divorce had stopped hurting, although some of what Kitty had said still lingered painfully, but talking about it would lead to deep waters.

The boat moved on and, looking back toward the shore, he said, "Tell me more about Stranahan House. What makes it so special anyway?"

"The man who built it is credited with being the founding father of Fort Lauderdale." She visibly relaxed, turning to face him, her hands falling to rest on her lap. "It was built in the early nineteen-hundreds…"

As she gave him a mini-history lesson David took it all in—although it was less the story and more the sound of her voice and her expressive face that held his attention. When she'd finished the story, he said, "You know a lot about the history of the city."

"I like history," she replied. "If I hadn't gone into nursing I'd probably have become a teacher."

He could see her doing that—interacting with the kids, enjoying watching their young minds soaking up knowledge and growing.

"Why didn't you go into pediatrics? You obviously love kids."

"Aw, hell no." Even though she chuckled, she didn't sound amused. "My heart couldn't stand it. Give me an adult in pain and I'm fine, but if it's a child or, worse, a baby… I turn into a mess. My peds rotation was the hardest on me emotionally." She shook her head slowly, her face taking on a faraway expression. "I almost quit nursing."

"I'm glad you didn't." Talking about it seemed to be taking her to a dark place—one he wondered at. "It was that bad, huh?"

"Yes, it was."

She was still facing him, but David wondered if she was even seeing him.

"There were a couple of days that left me wondering what it was all about—if there was any reason to try to help. If it wasn't for Aliya, I'd probably have snapped."

He knew what she was talking about. He'd experienced some of those same emotions during his residency—times when he'd seen the worst human beings could do, and his faith and optimism had been stretched to breaking point.

Not wanting her to relive those hard times, he instinctively stroked her hand and said, "This must have been a fun place to grow up."

She shrugged, leaving her hand where it was, beneath his. "I know it was for some people. I didn't have the chance to enjoy it until I was older."

Another sore subject. He could tell by the way her fingers clenched into a fist. But this one he didn't want to skirt. "Why wasn't it for you?"

She glanced toward shore and he heard the sound of the boat's engines change. She'd said their stop was next, so hopefully she'd answer before they had to disembark.

Instead of answering, she asked, "You grew up poor, right?"

That was an understatement, but he simply said, "Yes."

"So what did you do during the summer?" Nychelle raised her eyebrows. "Probably worked, right?"

"Yes." He nodded slowly, wondering what she was getting at. "I helped my dad in his shop, and picked up whatever other jobs I could."

"What else? Did your family spend some time together? Were there times when you got to do other stuff?"

"Sure." Wasn't that what childhood was all about? She seemed to be waiting for him to elaborate, so he continued, "When we were little Mary-Liz, Donny, our cousins, and I spent as much time as we could outdoors. Every now and then, when our parents could afford it, we'd spend a day at the beach or go camping. When I was a little older I'd save up my money to go to science camp."

His parents had let him, instead of insisting he use the money to buy school supplies, although he'd done that too. Talking about it with Nychelle, he suddenly realized it had been a childhood of joy and wonder, despite the poverty.

"Sounds like hard work, but with fun to balance it out." She tipped her chin up in an almost combative gesture. "For us—Olivia and me—everything was geared toward our futures in medicine, being prepared to get into the best colleges and *'getting a leg up on the competition.'*"

The way she enunciated the last words told him it was something she'd heard often.

"There wasn't much room for good times under those circumstances." She gently pulled her hand out from under his and reached for her bag. "We get off here."

As they waited for the boat to dock he contemplated what she'd said. It wasn't hard to believe. Having met her parents, he could imagine the pressure they'd put on their children. He'd gone to school with some people he suspected had been raised in a similar way. If they hadn't got one hundred percent on a test, or aced a subject during a semester, they'd freaked, worried about what their parents would say. He'd even seen some of them crack under the strain, and knowing that made him admire Nychelle all the more. It must have taken immense strength of character to stand up to her parents and go her own way.

He'd had to work like a fiend to get to medical school—but not because his parents had been pushing him. For him it had been work to secure scholarships, to have enough money to get where he wanted to go. It was ironic to feel bad for Nychelle, knowing she'd come from such a wealthy family, and yet she had missed out on the joys of childhood because her parents were so single-minded.

"Well," he said finally, as they stood on the dock waiting for the other water taxi to come so they could continue their adventure, "why don't we make up for some of that lost time?"

Brow wrinkled, she asked, "What?"

"The fun times you missed as a kid." He grinned. "Let's make up for them."

The beginnings of a smile tugged at her lips. "How do you suggest we do that?"

"Personally, all *my* childish fantasies involved ice cream and clothes that were bought specifically for me. What did you wish you could do in summers back then?"

Even behind the dark lenses of her glasses he could see her eyes widen.

"I don't know," she replied quickly, but then she shook her head. "I do know. I wanted to go to the beach and build sandcastles, or go to a water park." She gave a little chuckle. "I was even jealous of my friends who complained they had to spend their vacations with their grandparents."

David took her hand. "Well, if you give me ice cream I'll build sandcastles with you. I'm pretty good at it, if I might say so myself. And if you don't believe me we can call my niece and nephew to have them verify that fact."

There was a moment of stillness between them, but David could feel Nychelle's gaze almost drilling into him, as though she didn't know how to react to his nonsense. And then she laughed: a full-bodied, throaty sound, echoing with what sounded like pure joy.

"You're on," she said, giving his fingers a squeeze. "And your skills had better not disappoint."

"Oh, they won't." He gave her a jaunty grin for good measure, feeling lighter, happier than the simple moment really called for. "I promise."

CHAPTER FOURTEEN

HOW HAD SHE ever questioned David's character? He was one of the nicest people she'd ever known.

Leaning back on her towel, Nychelle watched as he added another tower to the sandcastle, expertly shaping it into a cylinder before starting to embellish it with crenellations.

"The trick is the amount of water you put in," he said, then glanced over at her and held up one sandy hand. "Aren't you going to help at all?"

Nychelle just chuckled and got up to shift the umbrella so it covered him better. "There. I helped stop you getting sunburned."

"Ha-ha." David shook his head and went back to decorating the castle with arrow slits inscribed into the sand with the end of his straw. "I thought this was something *you* wanted to do."

He tried to sound disgruntled, but couldn't stop the sides of his lips quirking, which spoiled the effect completely.

"I'm finding watching you even more fun than I'd have actually doing it. Besides, you're so much better at it than I could ever be."

His laughter brought a smile to her lips as she resumed her seat beneath the other umbrella and tucked her legs up under her. It was, she decided, the best day she could ever have hoped for. Simple pleasures, enjoyed together.

They'd floated along the Intracoastal, looking at the fabulous houses, critiquing the architecture and marveling at the luxuriousness of the surroundings and the boats berthed outside many of the residences. Initially Nychelle had planned for them to have lunch at one of her favorite waterside restaurants, but the smell of the seafood had made her feel queasy as soon as they'd walked in. David hadn't commented or complained when she'd changed her mind, and they'd strolled along for a couple of blocks more, until they'd found an up-scale burger joint.

Although their conversation had been light enough, she'd discovered a few things she hadn't known before. He'd talked a bit more about his marriage and, in true David fashion, had spoken of his ex with respect and regret, rather than acrimony.

Thinking the woman a fool for letting him go, Nychelle had wanted to ask for more details. But when he'd moved on to talk about something else she hadn't pressed the subject. After all, it had been her idea not to go too deep today.

After lunch they'd wandered along South Fort Lauderdale Beach Boulevard, browsing shop windows and craft stalls. He'd threatened to buy her an alligator foot keychain or a gator tooth necklace, both of which she'd politely refused through her laughter. But she'd stopped on her way back from the ladies' room and bought him a tropical print shirt in colors so wild she was sure he'd never wear it.

He had immediately put it on.

"Good grief!" she'd said, breathless from giggling. "I don't know if I want to be seen with you in that."

"Too bad," he'd replied, with a grin that just turned her insides to mush. "You should have thought of that before you bought it."

Then, true to their agreement, she'd bought him an ice cream cone, which had prompted him to suggest they cross over to the beach and build their sandcastle. With one more stop to get another round of cold drinks, they'd done just that.

It was surprising to realize the sun was sinking toward the horizon already, although it wouldn't get dark until after six.

"The day has flown by." She suppressed a sigh, wishing their time together could last longer. "We should think about heading back soon."

He looked up and gave a one-shouldered shrug. "If I wasn't so covered in sand I'd suggest making an evening of it, but I'm not fit to go anywhere like this."

Nychelle nodded in agreement. While it hadn't been very windy, the sea breeze had left her feeling salty and sticky. "You can explore the night-life another time."

Slanting her a quick glance, he replied, "Yes, we can."

Busying herself by pulling out her phone, Nychelle ignored his comment. "I need to take a picture of the sandcastle. It's amazing."

"One second." Using his straw, David wrote around the inside of the moat in neat script: *Queen Nychelle's Palace.*

"You're a disgrace to the medical profession, having handwriting that neat," Nychelle teased as she snapped several pictures, including a couple that featured him rather than the sandcastle.

"I don't believe in conforming to other people's expectations." He stood up and brushed at his sand-covered legs, with little effect.

"True," she said as she gathered up her bag. "Not doing so really does make life interesting."

She knew that for sure, having spent years doing what she felt was right for her rather than what others wanted.

She just wished she knew whether spending all this time with David was a good thing or not.

It had been an easy, uncomplicated day on the surface, but every time he'd smiled, or reached out to hold her hand, Nychelle had been aware of the undercurrents. As swift and strong as a riptide, they were rife with attraction, both physical and emotional—at least for her. Wishing she knew how he felt about it was futile. She wouldn't ask. Not only because she was leery of actually knowing, but because she didn't want to risk spoiling the day.

It had been wonderful.

Yet as they walked toward the shower at the exit near the road Nychelle looked back at the sandcastle and felt a sharp pang of sadness, knowing that it, like the day, would soon be gone.

Maybe it was the sun, or perhaps the amount of laughing he'd done during their day out, but as they wound their way back toward the water taxi stop David felt mellow. Happily tired. Nychelle looked pensive, though, and he could only hope it was because, like him, she was regretting the end of their time together.

As they hurried across the busy street toward the Intracoastal, where they'd catch the water taxi, he took her hand again. She gave his fingers a squeeze, then slanted him a glance.

"Why did you decide on general practice instead of a specialty?"

The question took him aback, and his first impulse was to avoid it. "Why did you? I would have thought with your family connections you would have gone in a different direction."

"Oh, no, you don't." She gave his hand a shake in emphasis. "Didn't anyone tell you answering a question with a question is an obvious sign of deflection? Why would you be defensive about something so simple?"

He groaned. "Analyzing me again?"

"Asking another question?" she shot back.

"Okay…okay."

He changed his grip on her hand, lacing his fingers with hers. It wasn't that he didn't want to tell her, just that he was sure she'd think he was nuts.

"I've always thought that eventually I'd want to move back to South Carolina and set up a practice near where my parents are. There aren't enough doctors in the area, and the hospital is a ways away—especially for some of the more rural communities."

He struggled to find the appropriate words.

"The people support each other every way they can, and my family benefited from that way of thinking. It's what neighbors do there, even when they have little themselves, so I've always wanted to give back."

He didn't tell her about the charity he'd been saving toward setting up since he'd first started making decent money, or that he had been talking to Dr. Hamatty about how he arranged his free clinics, hoping to do something similar one day. Yet even without that the look she gave him, so full of admiration and joy, made him feel as though he were suddenly ten feet tall.

"How lovely. I think that's wonderful!"

She beamed, as if he'd given her a gift, and his heart ached, feeling suddenly too big for its place in his chest.

There was nothing he could say; his throat was tight with emotion. During the day he'd opened up to her more than he had to anyone else for a long time, speaking about his parents and siblings, and the home he'd run from and yet often longed for. Even about Kitty, although he hadn't been able to bring himself to say why the marriage had failed.

That was a conversation he thought might happen soon, but he'd prefer to have it somewhere other than in public.

He wasn't sure he wouldn't break down telling her about Natalie. Even though time had made the pain more bearable, there was something about Nychelle that brought all his emotions close to the surface. As though she were some kind of magnet, which drew from him all he sought to hide or hide from.

They were near the dock when Nychelle said, "Whoops!" Tightening her grip on his hand, she continued, "Look. The next taxi is coming. Let's go."

She broke into a run and he fell in with her, the sound of her laughter, the gleam of her smile, making that sweet ache in his chest expand, filling him with contentment.

Breathless, they threw themselves onto a bench at the prow of the boat, exchanging smiles.

"Just a moment! Please—just a moment!"

At the shout from the dock David looked up and saw the same family they'd shared the trip with that morning running toward the boat, the two older members bringing up the rear. The taxi waited, and one after the other they clambered onto the boat, the adults red-faced with exertion.

This wasn't the calm, happy group of the morning, David thought. The older children were obviously exhausted and, as often happened with siblings, were squabbling and baiting one another. The father was now holding the baby, who squealed in outrage, while the mother and grandparents corralled all the various bits and pieces the family had needed for their excursion.

After watching them get settled—which involved the stowing of equipment, the swapping of the baby from hand to hand, and a few sharp words to the older kids from Dad—David turned to Nychelle with a wry grin.

"I always tip my hat to parents. Just watching the chaos sometimes makes me tired."

His own words took him by surprise. Normally he avoided any reference to children, and any jokes about what parents went through, since they brought with them regrets for what he was missing.

"It's wonderful chaos," she retorted, and there was an edge to her voice. "There's nothing I love more than taking care of Leighann and MJ. It's crazy, but rewarding."

"No doubt it is." Her vehemence was startling, pulling him out of his own contemplation. "I didn't mean it as a—"

"I look forward to experiencing it."

Her interruption was fierce. Although she still spoke softly, all pretense of indifference was washed from her tone, and the hand she held up was defensive, as if she expected him to object or argue.

"I don't understand why children are suddenly seen as a burden—something to be put off and a cause of problems in peoples' lives. No matter how chaotic, I think people should be *thankful* for their kids."

"They should be." That he knew for a fact. He took her hand, squeezed gently, wanting to calm her.

"Some aren't, though."

Now she just sounded sad, rather than angry, and an ache formed in David's chest.

"It's sad when so many people are longing for kids and can't have them. I can't wait to be a mother."

As she pushed her sunglasses firmly up on her nose and turned to look out over the water David was left wondering. Was that a general observation about infertility, or was she thinking of someone specific? Perhaps herself?

Before he could decide how to best broach the subject Nychelle rolled her shoulders, as though sloughing off the conversation. She drew in a deep breath and turned to him, smiling a somewhat wobbly smile.

"So, what do you think of Fort Lauderdale now you've seen a bit more of it? How does it compare to Chicago?"

He had no choice but to follow her lead, and yet her remark about longing for children of her own had cast a shadow over the day. Over his heart. She had no idea how that drive to be a parent, the longing to bring another life into the world, could cause an agony beyond anything she'd ever experienced.

The ache in his chest intensified, and even as he answered her question he felt the peace he'd only just experienced evaporate in the glare of the setting sun.

Nychelle's need to be a mother put paid to any hopes of him being anything more to her than just a friend. And that hurt more than he wanted to admit even to himself.

CHAPTER FIFTEEN

NYCHELLE'S HEART WAS POUNDING, and a sour taste settled at the back of her throat as David talked about the comparative merits of the two most recent cities he'd lived in. She nodded at what seemed to be the appropriate times, although she was only minimally following what he was saying.

What on earth had come over her to go on a rant like that?

But she knew what had caused her to lose her cool. David was, in her opinion, perfect father material. He was kind, calm, beautiful of spirit. The knowledge that he didn't want kids rankled. And when he'd seemed to be denigrating parenthood altogether…

She was overreacting. Also, *she* was the one who had imposed the rule about not discussing anything intimate, and she had broken it.

There was no way she could continue on the way they were. Too much simmered between them. Over the last few weeks she'd grown more and more intrigued by him, had felt attraction smoldering beneath her skin. Today had fanned it into a wildfire. He was all she'd ever wanted in a man. Yet once he knew she was pregnant there would be nothing left between them—maybe not even friendship—so she wanted to get it over with. Deal with it now rather than later, as Aliya had so wisely counseled.

It was hard to find the words, though, hard to trust him with her news, even though in her heart she knew it was the right thing, and they switched over to the New River line in silence.

The loss of camaraderie was no doubt her fault, and she withdrew into herself, trying to come up with the right words to make her decisions make sense to him the way they had to her.

Finally she turned to David, still unsure, but determined to do the right thing. "Listen," she said, having to stop and clear her tight throat before she could continue. "I feel as though I owe you an explanation."

He raised his hand, but she didn't let him interrupt. If he said it was okay, she'd probably wimp out.

"From when I was a little girl I loved babies and other children. The ladies who looked after Olivia and I used to call me *Little Momma*."

She pronounced it *Lilli Mumma*, the Jamaican way, out of habit, and saw him smile.

"I would get up before school and go to check on Olivia before I got dressed or had my breakfast. It just came naturally to me. I wanted to make sure she was okay, and felt as though it was my job to ensure she was. I was even like that with Aliya—which annoyed the heck out of her, since she's actually a couple months older than me."

David leaned back, his intense focus on her causing distracting shivers to run across her shoulders and down her arms, as happened every time she had his full concentration.

"So you've wanted to be a mother from when you were a little girl?"

"Yes." She nodded, facing him head-on rather than looking away, the way she really wanted to. Their stop was coming up. People were rising, preparing to get off the boat. There might not be enough time to tell him everything she wanted to.

"But there's more to it than that. You see, when I was thirteen I developed dysfunctional uterine bleeding. Eventually, because medication wasn't working, I ended up having a D&C and there was some scarring. The doctors warned I may never get pregnant."

The boat bumped the dock and people crowded around, getting closer to the exit point. Suddenly self-conscious about airing her personal business in public, she stopped talking. David was still staring at her, and she wished she could understand his expression, but he was keeping it carefully neutral; it was his professional face, as if she were a patient.

Tension making her feel almost nauseated, she got up. "Can we finish this conversation later?"

"Sure," he replied.

But his gaze lingered on her face, making heat climb up her neck and into her cheeks.

The family group, which had changed over to the second water taxi with them, were getting ready to disembark too, and she turned to watch them. The father had taken hold of the older kids, helping the eldest put on his knapsack and carrying the other one. Mom juggled the now squirming baby and the ubiquitous diaper bag until the older lady said, "Let me take the nappy bag," and relieved her of it.

As the younger woman said, "Thanks, Deana," the older gentleman reached for the stroller, which had been folded up and stowed beneath the bench.

"I've got the buggy," he said.

Nychelle was about to comment to David on the older folks' English accents when the older man straightened, stroller in hand, took a staggering step back and then collapsed.

For a moment everything seemed to slow as the elderly

man fell backward, and then she heard the *crack* of his head hitting the bench on the other side of the water taxi.

"George!"

The older woman was a step ahead of Nychelle, and fell to her knees beside the man's crumpled body. She grabbed his shoulders, but Nychelle held on to her hands, stopping her from shaking the unconscious man.

"Wait—"

"I'm a doctor." David was there, bending down, already reaching for the patient's wrist. "Let me take a look."

"Give us some room," Nychelle said to the woman, hoping she'd back away. When she only continued crying out her husband's name, and wouldn't release her grip on his shoulders, Nychelle turned to the rest of the family, who were standing as if turned to stone. "Someone help this lady up. And call 911 immediately."

There was a flurry of activity: the younger man rushed forward to pull the distraught woman away, one of the deckhands shouted to the captain to tell him what had happened. As soon as the other woman was out of her way Nychelle concentrated on the patient. He was partially seated, slouched against the base of the bench, held up by a jut in the gunwale.

"Pulse is elevated, but strong. Respiration within normal range. Pupils responsive." David straightened from his examination. "Stabilize his head. Let's get him flat on the deck."

Nychelle did as she was told, holding the gentleman's head and neck while David supported his upper torso, so as to shift him away from the bench without risking any additional injury to his spine.

"Gently. Gently…" he said. "And down we go."

As soon as they had the gentleman flat, Nychelle said, "Scalp laceration," although she was sure David would have noticed the blood on the bench, and the spreading pool on the deck where the man's head now lay.

David reached around to palpate the wound. "No obvious sign of fracture." He straightened. "Apply pressure."

None of the towels in her bag was clean, so Nychelle looked over her shoulder at the baby's parents. "Give me a clean diaper. Hurry."

The mother moved first, bending to scrabble in the bag for one, handing it over with a shaking hand.

Folding it inside out to create a pad, Nychelle pressed it to the wound, glad they didn't need to lift the man's head for her to do so.

David leaned closer to the gentleman. "George? George? Can you hear me?"

When there was no response, he flicked his finger on the patient's cheek and called to him again. It was only on the third try that George's eyelids fluttered and he moaned.

When his eyes opened a crack, David said, "Hey, there. You're all right, but stay still for me."

"Wh-what happened?"

Despite David's injunction for him to stay still George made a move to sit up, and David stopped him with a hand on his chest.

"Where am I?"

"You fell and hit your head. The ambulance is on its way, but I need you to stay still." David's calm voice had the patient relaxing, although his face was lined with pain. "Can you answer a few questions for me?"

"Y-yes." George scrunched his eyes closed for a moment, but then opened them slightly again.

"How old are you?"

"Eighty-three," he replied, with only a fractional hesitation before the words.

"Do you have a heart condition?"

"No. High blood pressure, though. Take pills for that."

"Any other medications?"

"No." He squeezed his eyes closed again, and a little groan followed his reply.

"Where does it hurt, George?"

"Have a cracking headache. And someone's using a damned blowtorch on my leg."

"Left or right?"

"Left."

Nychelle was glad to hear the distant sound of approaching sirens. There was only so much they could do for this gentleman. David had asked George to move his leg, and although he could a bit, it obviously caused him a lot of pain. Nychelle suspected a broken hip and, while most people might assume the fall had caused the break, she knew that more often than not the break actually happened first, causing the fall. Many older people weren't aware of the dangers of bone loss caused by aging and other chronic, sometimes undiagnosed, conditions until a situation like this one arose.

Having finished his exam, David offered no opinion other than to say, "The ambulance should be here any minute. Would you like your wife to keep you company until the paramedics get here? She's been very worried about you."

"Yes." George's English accent was even more pronounced than before. "Let her see I'm not done for yet."

David looked over to where the rest of family were all huddled together on the dock. Everyone but a deckhand had disembarked in preparation for the EMTs' arrival. "What's her name?"

"Deana."

Nychelle knew that with each question and reply David was testing the injured man's mental abilities.

"Pretty name," David said, eliciting a small smile from the patient.

When David called and gestured to Deana, the deckhand helped her back on board and she hurried over. Kneeling beside her husband, she grabbed his nearest hand.

"It's all right, darling." George tried to be reassuring, although his voice was weak. "Just a little fall."

"What happened to him?" Deana asked David, her voice quavering. "Was it a heart attack?"

"The ambulance is on its way. They'll be able to better tell you what happened when he gets to the hospital."

"Why won't *you* tell me?" Her voice rose beseechingly. "You said you were a doctor. You should know what's happened. I need to know what's happened to my husband—"

"Stop it, Dee." George's voice was firm, and he gave his wife's hand a little shake. "Enough. The poor doc was just having a nice day out with his lady. I doubt he has a stethoscope or any other equipment hidden in his shorts, do you?"

His voice was a little breathy, and Nychelle was relieved that the wail of the ambulance had stopped. The EMTs should be there soon. The diaper was already heavy with blood, and Nychelle could see the first signs of incipient shock; George had paled, his respirations were quickening, and a touch of his face revealed he was clammy.

"It's okay, George." David was as calm as ever. "Deana, here come the paramedics. They're going to need you to go back onto the dock so they can do their job."

Instead of moving Deana added her other hand to the clasp she had on her husband. "No. I—"

It wasn't unusual to have family members be more difficult than the patients, so Nychelle tamped down her frustration. Looking Deana in the eyes, she said, "If you truly want to know what's happened to George, let the EMTs get him to the hospital as quickly as possible."

Perhaps it was her tone, or the seriousness of her expression. But something got through to the woman, who bent quickly to kiss her husband on the lips and then moved back toward the dock, just as the rattle of equipment heralded the paramedics' arrival.

"Forgive her," George muttered. "She's a firecracker. Always has been."

"It's fine," Nychelle replied in a reassuring tone. He'd grown even paler, and was beginning to shake. "Don't worry about it. It's not a big deal at all."

But she was still a bit steamed. She was used to having patients doubt her abilities—sometimes even rudely. It was part of the job, and it didn't bother her anymore. But somehow hearing someone seeming to question David's competence had just set her teeth on edge.

David rose, getting out of the way so the lead paramedic could take his place. As the EMT gave him a questioning look David introduced himself, then said, "Patient staggered and fell backward, striking his head. He was unconscious for approximately two minutes. Pulse and respiration are within normal range, although rapid. He sustained a scalp laceration and I suspect he also has a broken hip. With the way he fell, I'd check for neck fractures and TBI."

The second paramedic approached with a neck brace and backboard, and Nychelle scooted away, giving her room. The first paramedic was asking David more questions as the two EMTs worked in a coordinated rhythm to prepare George for his trip to the hospital.

There was nothing left for her to do, so Nychelle got up, gingerly picking up her bag as she did so, hoping not to get too much blood on it. Standing to one side, her attention wasn't on the paramedics or their patient. It was all on David: on his expression as he watched the EMTs fit George with the neck brace and backboard, on the timbre of his voice as he answered their questions. She was fascinated by the way his long fingers flexed, as though his capable, beautiful hands wanted to get back to helping the patient, and then by how quickly he moved to assist the paramedics lifting George onto the stretcher.

He was a man made for his profession; his desire to diagnose, to heal, was ingrained into his soul. Yet it was just one part of him—an important facet, but just one of many that added up to the most amazingly perfect man she'd ever met.

Suddenly, just as the stretcher was being moved toward the dock, he looked up and caught her staring. In that moment, as their gazes met, the chaos seemed to subside and a sense of almost surreal calm enfolded her. The spark that zinged between them couldn't be denied even if she wanted to. It wasn't the aftermath of the incident making her knees weak and her heart leap. It was him. *All* him.

The stretcher rattled past her and Nychelle blindly turned to follow its path. She vaguely registered the family milling about and hurrying off after the paramedics.

Then David was beside her.

"Let's get out of here."

All thoughts of their prior conversation fled. She didn't ask where they were going—didn't ask any questions at all. She just nodded, knowing she'd go wherever he wanted.

CHAPTER SIXTEEN

SOMETHING HAD CHANGED between them. It had sparked in her eyes when she'd looked at him on the dock. It had shimmered like heat off asphalt between them during the walk back to his car, and it still hung in the air, strong enough to have the hair rising on his arms while he settled into the driver's seat.

"Come home with me," he said, breaking the silence, trying to gauge her reaction to his words from her clear-cut beautiful profile.

He had it in mind to add his apartment was closer than her house, and that although they'd paused at the restaurant to wash their hands, it would offer her the chance to clean up properly.

But as he was about to say all that Nychelle turned toward him. "Yes."

For a moment it was as though time itself held its breath. Then David's gaze dropped from Nychelle's eyes to her mouth, snagged there, entranced. She wasn't smiling. Instead the curve of her lips was a little shy, but also knowing. It was like a siren's call…irresistible. Yet he didn't move, exerted a superhuman effort not to lean forward and kiss her the way he so desperately wanted to. If he did, he wouldn't be able to stop.

Instead he pressed the start button on the car and turned

his thoughts, as best he could, to backing out of the parking space. Neither of them spoke as he turned out of the parking structure and drove east toward his condominium, which was ten minutes away.

The radio played softly. The song was one David had in the past thought illustrated an unrealistic ideal—one in which a man loved all the different facets of his woman, even the imperfections. Now he heard it with different ears, tuned to a new frequency that understood what the crooning singer meant.

There was nothing about Nychelle he disliked, and so much that he admired. The tenacity and courage she'd displayed in following her own path in life, not the one everyone had seemed to expect of her. The reticence she hid behind her warm, engaging smile, which was unusual in these days when people overshared their every thought and feeling. He liked it. Being forced to dig beneath the surface to understand her and get to know what she thought important in life was exhilarating. Over and over he'd found new things to respect about her, including her grace in the face of her parents' disapproval and the calm, friendly way she interacted with patients and colleagues.

He'd fought so hard to resist the attraction between them, but now, with the knowledge that she was unlikely to be able to conceive, that resistance was melting away.

It was so selfish of him to feel her infertility was a sign, but he did. He hurt for her, knowing how much she wanted to be a mother. And if he were honest he wanted children too, but couldn't seem to get past his fear that somehow Natalie not making it to term had been his fault. Kitty had remarried, and now had two children with her new husband, all born without problems. Intellectually he knew it probably wasn't the case, but he wasn't willing to take the risk.

He was beginning to feel as though eventually he might

be able to handle being a father through adoption, if it meant having Nychelle. Because having Nychelle in his life permanently would be heaven.

It took no effort to imagine her at his side, in his bed. He wanted to take her to South Carolina to meet his family, who he was sure would adore her as much as he did. Wanted to have her early-morning smiles, or her grumpiness if it turned out she wasn't a morning person, and her goodnight kisses. Wanted to see her face as she lost herself in ecstasy and know he was the one who'd given her pleasure.

The longing that last image conjured was a physical ache in his belly. And lower.

Was this love? He was sure it was. The song he'd previously dismissed as sentimental now made perfect sense. No doubt Nychelle had her faults—although if someone asked right now he wouldn't be able to name one—but no matter what they were, he couldn't see them making a difference to how he felt. He'd never been more certain about anything in his life. To him Nychelle was perfect—and perfect for him.

Pulling into the apartment complex, he drove around to the entrance to the underground parking lot and pushed the button to open the gate. Nychelle still hadn't spoken, but a quick peep at her showed nothing but serenity in the lines of her face. As he drove down the ramp he thought it seemed as though she'd come to a decision and was at peace with it. If only he knew what that decision was…

Trying not to wonder about that propelled him into speech. "The apartment isn't much. I rented it furnished and haven't made many changes. But it does have a really nice view from the balcony. I thought we could order in some food and just relax after that excitement with George."

Pulling into his space, he put the car in Park and turned to look at Nychelle, just as she slanted him a glance from the corner of her eye.

"Mmm-hmm," she replied, with a little quirk of her lips. "That sounds good."

He took her hand on their way to the elevator, and when he heard her indrawn breath he knew he wasn't the only one who felt the electric charge generated by the connection of his skin with hers. He tightened his fingers around hers, swept his thumb across the back of her hand, reveling in the softness of her, longing to feel her touch on his skin again.

They rode up to his floor in silence, and he resented having to release her hand to unlock his door. Need built beneath his skin, tightening his muscles, making it difficult for him to breathe normally. As they stepped inside he knew he should wait, but couldn't.

As soon as the door closed behind them he drew her into his arms. Reaching up, he took off her sunglasses and set them, along with his own, on the hall table.

"David…" It was a sigh: arousal, surrender and fear all intermingled. She looked vulnerable, and his heart twisted. "We shouldn't…"

Cupping her face, he said, "Maybe not." A light, lingering kiss sealed whatever she was planning to say next behind her lips, and as she melted against him, trembling, he lifted his mouth just far enough away to say, "But unless you tell me you don't want me I don't want to stop—consequences be damned."

"I…"

Her attempt at a reply ended on a muffled sound, rife with desire, as he trailed his lips to her ear and nipped the lobe.

"Tell me you don't want me, Nychelle."

He whispered it in her ear, felt a shiver race through her body. Her nipples pressed, tightly furled, against his chest, demanding attention.

"Tell me to stop and I will."

* * *

Nychelle tried with all her might to say they shouldn't go any further, but couldn't get the words out. Knowing she needed to tell him the rest of her story battled with the desire making her head swim and her body tingle and thrum with desire.

"Tell me you don't want me," he said again, and she knew she couldn't. To do so would be to lie.

"I can't. You know I can't. But…"

He didn't wait to hear the rest, just took her mouth in a kiss that made what she'd planned to say fly right out of her brain.

Desire flared, hotter than the Florida sun, and Nychelle surrendered to it, unable and unwilling to risk missing this chance to know David intimately, even if it were just this once. Was it right? Wrong? She couldn't decide—didn't want to try to.

There were so many more things she should explain to him, but she knew she wouldn't. Telling him about the baby when she knew he didn't want a family would destroy whatever it was growing between them. It was craven, perhaps even despicable not to be honest with him, and she hated herself for being underhand, but her mind, heart and body were at war, and she'd already accepted which would win.

She'd deal with the fallout, whatever it might be, tomorrow. Today—this evening—she was going to have what she wanted, live the way she wanted. Enjoy David for this one time. There would only be regrets if she didn't.

His lips were still on hers, demanding, delicious. She'd relived the kisses they'd shared over and over in her mind, but now she realized memory was only a faded facsimile of reality. The touch and taste and scent of him encompassed her, overtaking her system on every level. Her desperate hands found their way beneath his shirt, and his groan of pleasure was as heartfelt as her joy at the first sensation of his bare skin beneath her palms.

His hands, in turn, explored her yearning flesh, stroking her face, then her neck. When they brushed along her shoulders, easing the straps of her sundress away, Nychelle arched against him. With a tug, he lowered her bodice and the bandeau-style bathing suit beneath it to her waist, and she rubbed her nipples against his chest, spurring him on, want turning to aching need within her.

Perhaps he felt the same way, for suddenly it was as though they had both lost all restraint. Arms tight around each other, their bodies moved in concert, their fiercely demanding kisses whipping the flames of arousal to an inferno.

Naked. She wanted him naked.

She set about achieving her goal, tugging at his shirt until they were forced to part so as to get it off over his head. Once it was out of the way David's lips came back to hers, and she breathed in the scent of him, the essence of it rising to her head, making her love-drunk. Already she had the knot of his board shorts untied, but she paused to cup the hard length of his erection through the fabric, a shiver racing along her spine, eagerness firing in its wake.

He made a sound in the back of his throat—something feral, predatory—and her legs almost gave way, trembling with anticipation. He lifted her, carried her easily into the bedroom, where he set her down on the bed. With swift, capable movements he stripped off her clothes, leaving her exposed. When his intent blue gaze stroked from her toes up to her head she felt it like a touch, and her body tightened even further, trembling with arousal.

Burning. She was burning from the inside out. She cried out as he fanned the flames of her excitement with his lips and hands, the slide of his body against hers. His mouth branded her breasts, her belly. His tongue slid and flicked over what felt like every inch of her torso, teasing and arousing, until she shook and writhed and yearned, caught on the edge of orgasm, slipping toward the chasm with every intent-filled touch he placed upon her body.

"You are so beautiful, Nychelle."

His torso was wedged between her thighs. His breath rushed over her belly, leaving a little trail of goose bumps. When he kissed her navel, swirling his tongue around the edge, her hips lifted and a pleading gasp left her throat. He smiled slightly, that beloved tilt of his lips, and although his lids were slumberous his eyes were dark, gleaming, and she felt his need vibrating through his body into hers.

"David," she pleaded. "Please. I want—"

He didn't let her finish—had already slid down as she spoke. And at the first touch of his lips on her most intimate flesh, the first swipe of his tongue through her folds, she shattered, crying out his name. Not a plea now, but a capitulation. A wild giving of herself—completely, utterly—even as she took the ecstasy he so freely gave and demanded…

"More…"

CHAPTER SEVENTEEN

DAVID FLOATED UP from a deep sleep and had one of those moments when, because of the quality of the light, he wasn't sure whether it was morning or evening. Then he took a deep breath, intending to yawn, but stopped as Nychelle's scent flooded his head.

'More...'

He heard her voice again in his head and, rolling onto his stomach, pulled her pillow over to bury his face in it. There had been more—and more. Lovemaking so intense, so utterly beautiful, a sensation of repletion filled him at the memory.

If he were a rooster, he'd crow as he remembered watching her straddle his body, taking him deep, her face tight with need. He'd cupped her breasts and she'd covered his hands with her own as she rocked above him, the connection between them so sublime it had thrown him into an altered state. One where all that mattered was Nychelle, the love swelling inside him, and her pleasure.

She'd cried out his name as her body had clutched his, her ripples of ecstasy catapulting him into an orgasm that had left him weak with pleasure. Just as the next one and the next one had, each pulling him further into love with her, making the bond between them grow stronger.

Thinking about it made him want to make love with

her all over again, although his stamina, as evidenced by his renewed erection, frankly astonished him. It was all her. Looking at her was aphrodisiac enough, but when he touched her, felt her touch in return, he reached a whole different level of arousal.

Where *was* she?

The bathroom door was open, but the door leading to the living room was almost completely closed. Sitting up, he reached for a pair of shorts and hoped she was out there ordering dinner. He was ravenous. Plus, he needed more energy for when he pulled her back into bed.

Stepping into the living room, he found her standing by the sliding door to the balcony, gazing out over the city lights. She'd found his bathrobe, which had been hanging on the back of his bedroom door, and he was glad she hadn't got dressed.

It would only mean undressing her all over again.

About to cross the room and embrace her from behind, he hesitated, something about her posture stopping him in his tracks. She turned, and her bleak expression made his heart stumble.

"Nychelle? What is it?"

"I have something to tell you. Something I should have told you before I… I slept with you."

"Okay…" But his throat felt tight, the word coming out rough and low.

Even from across the room he could see her inhale, and he already knew, from the habitual rubbing of her wrist, that whatever she had to say probably wouldn't be good.

"I had IUI a few weeks ago. I'm pregnant."

The words hung in the air and he was unable to make sense of them immediately. Reaching behind him, he found the arm of the couch with one hand and sat down before his trembling legs gave out.

That couldn't be right, could it?

"But you said…"

What had she said? His brain scrambled to remember.

"I developed dysfunctional uterine bleeding. The doctors warned I may never get pregnant."

She hadn't said she couldn't, just that she might never.

Everything inside him froze, ice filling his chest and spreading into his veins. Desperate, not wanting her to see what she was doing to him, he donned a stoic, neutral mask.

Her lips trembled slightly, and her eyes grew liquid with tears. "I'm sorry. I should have told you. I just—"

"It was none of my business." The distance in his tone made the words hollow. The breath caught in his throat, painful and raw, and had to be forcefully expelled before he could say, "I understand."

"Do you?"

It was, to him, a moot point. One he didn't want to discuss.

He would have told her so, but she said, "I don't think you do, and I'd like to explain."

He lifted his hand, gesturing for her to go on, humoring her, and for an instant he saw a hint of what might be anger in her eyes. Then it faded, and she sighed. Moving to the dining table, she pulled out a chair and sank into it. All this he watched as if from a distance, detached, refusing to allow himself to get pulled in. To feel.

"Two years ago I discovered that my fiancé, Nick, was cheating on me. He'd told me that while he eventually wanted kids he wasn't ready yet, and I'd agreed to wait. Then I found out the woman he'd been cheating with was pregnant. He tried to say it was a mistake, get me to take him back, but I think that was because he was worried my father would be angry."

She shrugged and shook her head, ruefulness evident in the gesture.

"Daddy didn't care, of course, and I won't bore you with

the rest of the fallout, but needless to say I was reluctant to get involved with anyone else after that."

David forced himself to nod—a sharp, get-on-with-it motion—and Nychelle closed her eyes for a second. He swallowed, feeling bad for her but also hating how the woman he'd just made love with now seemed a perfect stranger.

Hating her for ruining the happiness he'd only just found.

"I didn't want to wait—take the chance of leaving the attempt to have a child until it was too late. With my problems there would always be risks, but the longer I waited, the longer the odds of my even conceiving would become. I didn't know..."

He winced, her words piercing the ice around his heart. What hadn't she known? That they'd meet? Fall...?

No. He couldn't think that way. Refused to. Wouldn't allow her to follow that train of thought in case she completely destroyed him. Instead, he asked the first question that came to mind. "What do your parents think about this?"

"They don't know. I didn't tell anyone except Aliya."

The sound that broke from her was bitter, but he didn't let it weaken the barriers he'd already thrown up around his battered heart.

"When the doctor told me, at thirteen, about the problems I'd have carrying a child I started crying. And my mother..." She paused, her hands clenching into fists. "Do you know what she said to me?"

"What?"

"She said I shouldn't cry. That it was a chance for me to concentrate on my career without having to conform to what society deemed was my duty to procreate."

She looked away, but he saw the way she blinked, trying to hold back her tears.

"I remember wondering if she regretted having us, saw

us as burdens she was forced to bear. It explained why she was hardly around—why she left our care to others and was only interested in how we were doing academically. Was so cold and uncaring."

"Maybe she was just trying to spare you the pain of trying and not being able to conceive." The instinctive words broke from him, tearing at his throat as they passed. "Or the pain of carrying a baby only to lose it later."

She stared at him, eyes wide, and he saw the tracks left by her tears. "You don't know…"

"But I *do* know." Trying to push back the pain, keep his expression stoic, took everything he had inside. "And that's the advice I'd have given you…as a parent who's lost a child."

The shock of his words left Nychelle frozen except for her hand, which crept to cover her still-flat belly. David's eyes flicked as he followed the movement, and then rose to her face again.

"What?" she whispered, a horrible, aching sensation filling her chest. "Oh, David."

"Yes." His lips twisted. "My daughter was born at twenty weeks."

The way he said it wasn't lost on her, and tears filled her eyes again. He didn't see it as his wife having had a miscarriage, but as his daughter being born too early to survive.

"It's soul-destroying, Nychelle. Something you never get over. I wouldn't wish it on someone I hate, much less on someone I care about."

The air she'd just inhaled stuck in her lungs. All she could do was shake her head and blink to clear the tears from her eyes as the enormity of what she'd done crashed over her.

David had gone through hell, and she was bringing it all back to him. It was there in his pain-filled eyes, and in the way his fingers gripped the arm of the couch until they turned white.

"So maybe your mother was trying to shield you the only way she knew how." A muscle jumped in his jaw. "She knew the difficulty you faced, the potential heartbreak, and she tried to stop you from doing something you might regret even more than you'd regret not having a child."

"Don't say that!" The storm building in her was a maelstrom of pain and anger, and they were both there in the ferocity of her cry. "I'll never regret trying."

"Really?" David got to his feet so quickly Nychelle gasped at the rapid motion. "Even if—God forbid—something happens to your child?" He turned away, his shoulders rigid, his fists clenched. "Believe me, at that point you'll feel nothing more than regret and heartbreak."

She saw it so clearly then: David's desire never to be a father again was really his need never to take a chance on losing another child. And she knew now there was no hope for them.

None.

Blissful numbness overcame her and she welcomed it, knowing she couldn't bear to fall apart in front of him. Feeling distantly amazed that her legs held her, she stood and walked toward the bedroom, unsurprised when David said nothing; didn't even turn to watch her go. Collecting her clothes from beside the bed, averting her eyes from the place where she'd experienced the greatest pleasure of her life, she went into the bathroom, quietly closing the door behind her.

Only then did her hands start to shake, and it took her longer than usual to get her swimsuit on, and her sundress, and to undo her ponytail, finger-comb her snarled hair and secure it again.

By the time she got back to the living room David was in the kitchen, as though it was important to put the width of the island between them. Her bag was on the table by the door, instead of on the floor where she'd dropped it earlier, and she figured he'd put it there so she wouldn't waste time searching for it.

So she'd get going quicker.

"I'll drop you home."

There was that distant tone again, and it struck her straight in the heart, threatening the calm encasing her. "No. I'll call a cab." She held up her hand when he looked as though he might argue. "Really. It's okay."

There were so many things she wanted to say, but couldn't. So many questions, too, that she would keep to herself. She'd destroyed whatever they might have had—even friendship. She didn't have the right to ask anything more of him.

But as she put her hand on the door handle there was one thing she had to ask. It was, to her, too important to ignore.

"What is her name?"

His expression didn't change, as though he hadn't heard her, but then his eyebrows went up in query.

"Your daughter," she clarified. "What's her name?"

The silence that fell was so profound Nychelle's ears hummed with it, and it felt as though she'd sucked the air from the room with her question. David's expression cycled through pain to surprise, and then to an almost beatific calm.

"Natalie," he said, so softly she almost couldn't hear. Then his voice got stronger. "Her name is Natalie."

"Beautiful." Her voice hitched, and she knew her control was slipping.

Without another word she opened the door to step through. When it closed behind her the click of the lock snapping into place sounded suspiciously like the crack of her heart breaking.

CHAPTER EIGHTEEN

ALL NYCHELLE WANTED to do was pull the afghan up under her chin and go back to sleep, but the insistent ringing of the doorbell wouldn't let her. Rolling to sit up, she groaned, wanting to disappear for a little while and let the world go by without her.

She'd made it as far as her couch the evening before. Haunted by the conversation she'd had with David, she'd replayed it over and over in her mind. The numbness which had allowed her to leave his place without breaking down completely had lifted, and she'd cried long into the evening. The pain she'd felt as she'd recalled David talking about his daughter had been visceral, and she'd wept as though Natalie were her own—as though David's agony were her own.

Finally she'd forced herself to eat some yoghurt and fruit, although her stomach had threatened rebellion the entire time, and then had fallen asleep in the living room, her dreams bedeviled by images of David.

"What time is it anyway?" she groused as she blinked to try to clear the sleep from her eyes.

A glance at the kitchen clock made her wince. Nine o'clock was far later than she usually slept, but who on earth was at her house at that time on a Sunday morning without letting her know they were coming?

David.

Her heart hammered at the thought, but looking through the peephole in the door brought a mixture of shock and disappointment.

Quickly unlocking the door, she opened it.

"Aliya? What are you doing here?"

Her cousin stepped in, letting go of her bag as she did so, and grabbed Nychelle in a hard, sweet hug. Tears immediately threatened and had Nychelle wiggling out of the embrace. Aliya held on to her shoulders, kicking the door shut behind her.

"I was worried about you, so I grabbed the first available flight out of Hartsfield." Her dark eyes flashed and her usually smiling mouth was grim. "I'm glad I did. You've been crying."

"But why were you worried?" Nychelle forced a smile. "We spoke a couple days ago. You knew I was fine."

Turning Nychelle toward the living room, Aliya gave her a little shove. "Yeah, well, when I get a call from your Dr. Warmington, saying he knows you're upset and is worried about you, and your phone goes straight to voice mail all evening, of course I'm going to drop everything and come see what's going on."

Shock made Nychelle stumble, and she grabbed the back of the nearest chair for balance. "David called you? When?"

Aliya moved the blanket out of the way, then plopped down on the couch. She patted the seat beside her in invitation, but Nychelle ignored her, still too surprised to move.

Aliya sighed. "Yesterday—in the evening. I tried calling you afterward—"

"I'd turned off my phone." Nychelle waved her hand. That wasn't the important part. "What did he say?"

"Just that you'd had a really upsetting day and he was worried about you." When Nychelle made a rolling *go on* gesture with her hand, Aliya shrugged. "Seriously, that was it."

Forcing her trembling legs to move, and still holding on to the chair for support, Nychelle stepped around to sink down into the seat. "How did he get your number?"

"Does it matter?" Aliya raised one eyebrow.

"You flew all this way just because—"

Her cousin's raised hand and fierce expression were enough to have Nychelle snap her mouth shut.

"Listen, you need me—here I am."

Her face softened, and Nychelle turned away from the love shining in her eyes.

"You know if the situation were reversed you'd be at my side in a flash. Besides, that stiff upper lip nonsense comes from your father's side of the family. This side is all about making noise and garnering sympathy. That's what I'd be doing, so I figured I'd give you the chance to have at it—even though apparently there's nothing really wrong with you. What I want to know is, what happened to make him feel he needed to call me?"

It all came flooding back, overwhelming her, and Nychelle covered her face to hide her tears.

"Tell me," Aliya said softly.

The words poured out of Nychelle then: how wonderful the day had been, how she'd started telling him about her medical issues and had been interrupted by George's accident. Even how, as she'd watched David minister to the other man, she'd realized just how she felt about him.

"You're in love with him."

It wasn't a question, but Nychelle didn't want to go there with her cousin, so instead she blurted, "I slept with him."

"Oh."

Aliya's shocked expression would normally have made Nychelle laugh, but she couldn't summon any amusement.

"Before I told him about the baby."

"Oh..."

"And then he told me he'd lost a daughter when she was born at twenty weeks."

She couldn't bring herself to say his wife had miscarried—not when David so obviously saw it as a premature birth.

"My situation brought it all back to him. I saw it on his face, in his eyes—the fear and the agony. The regret. And I knew, no matter what had happened between us, it was over. He'd never take the chance of going through that again."

"Oh, honey." Aliya got up and came over to perch on the arm of the chair, pulled Nychelle into a hug. "You can't know that for certain. It was a shock, and once he's thought about it..."

"You didn't see him. He was gutted." Nychelle buried her head in her cousin's lap, tears flowing to dampen Aliya's dress. "He'll never forgive me. And I'll never forgive myself for hurting him that way."

Aliya sighed and stroked Nychelle's hair, seemingly unable to come up with a reply. After a while, she sighed again, then said, "Listen, you're upset, and probably overtired. Did you sleep much last night?" When Nychelle shook her head, Aliya coaxed her out of the chair and over to the couch. "Lie down for a while. I'm going to cook some soup."

"I'm not sick," Nychelle pointed out as she allowed her cousin to tuck the afghan over her legs. "I don't need soup."

"Maybe not, but cooking clears my head and I need to think about everything you've told me. And you need to eat. My goddaughter or godson needs nourishment, and Auntie Aliya is going to provide it."

Nychelle felt herself relax as the sound of her cousin bustling about in the kitchen filled the house. No matter how David had gotten Aliya's number, she was grateful he'd cared enough to make sure she wasn't alone. At the same time it was just more evidence of the kind of man he was, and the relationship she'd missed out on.

Shifting around so she was sitting up against the cushions, Nychelle said, toward the kitchen, "You can say it, you know."

Aliya glanced over her shoulder to ask, "Say what?"

"That you were right to tell me to wait."

Aliya put chicken in the pot. "I'll say *I told you so* if you want, but what good will that do?"

"I don't know. Maybe justify how horrible I feel about all of this?"

Aliya didn't answer immediately, and when she did her tone was musing. "If you had waited, and gotten involved with David, because of how he feels chances are you wouldn't even have tried to get pregnant. Is that what you would have wanted?"

"No!" Pushing herself farther up on the cushions, Nychelle glared at her cousin's back. "Of course not. I won't ever regret doing what I did."

"So, then, you're going to have to accept the situation as it is." Aliya's rueful and kindly tone softened the prosaic response. "It isn't like it's a binary situation, where you can only regret either trying for a baby *or* not being with David. You're going to have to deal with loving both the baby and David—even though it seems as if you can only have one but not the other."

Suddenly exhausted, ineffably sad, Nychelle slid back down on the couch and pulled the afghan up so only the top of her head was exposed.

"I kind of hate him right now," she mumbled, more to herself than to Aliya. "For being the perfect man and coming into my life at the worst possible time."

"No, you don't. It's yourself you're hating, and you need to stop. Poor David's probably as messed up about all this as you are."

It made sense. Too much sense. "I hate it when you're right." Sitting up, she grabbed a tissue and blew her nose in an effort to be able to breathe, but her next thought just made her tear up again. "I doubt he cares about me now."

"I don't know, honey, and neither do you. And you won't know until you talk to him. At least then you'll know for sure where you stand. You want to know that, don't you?"

It was on the tip of her tongue to deny even caring about where she stood with David Warmington, but they'd both know it was a lie. "Yes..."

Aliya chuckled at the grudging admission, then said, "Think about it. Talk to him when you're ready." When she continued, her voice was soft, yet serious. "I know you're in love with him, Nych, even if you won't come out and say it. You wouldn't have slept with him if you weren't. Maybe it's time to take stock, figure it all out, before you try to move on. He's all wrapped up with this period of your life, and sometimes you have to deal with everything that's happening rather than just bits and pieces."

"Okay, that's enough." Through her tears and stuffiness Nychelle found some laughter, let it roll over her. "You sound like a TV psychologist. Or your mom."

"Ha!" Aliya sounded suitably outraged. "Could be worse. I could sound like *your* mom."

Full-on giggles caused Nychelle almost to suffocate, since she still couldn't breathe through her nose. "That is too darn true."

He'd been unable to sleep, to eat, since Nychelle had left the night before, and finally David took his tortured mind and tired body down to the beach for a run. It made no sense for him to sit at home waiting for text updates from Nychelle's cousin. They obviously weren't coming. She'd been kind enough to let him know she was in Fort Lauderdale and on her way to Nychelle's house. He really couldn't expect more than that. After all, she didn't even know him.

But it didn't stop him from checking his phone every couple of minutes, anxiety like a tangle of barbed wire in his gut.

Pounding along the sand, he let the events of the last couple of days play over and over in his mind. It was surreal—life swinging from ecstatic to familiar nightmare in just a few hours.

Nychelle was pregnant. Not just pregnant but at high risk for miscarriage too.

Just the thought made him shiver, his skin pebbling with goose bumps despite the heat.

Hearing that had filled him with a fear so strong he'd felt nauseated. Memories of Natalie and the aftermath of her too-early birth had flooded his head; Kitty's screamed recriminations, coming at a time when he'd hardly been able to handle the loss of their baby. The slamming of the door when she'd left to go back to South Carolina, which had seemed to echo like a gunshot in his soul. The agonizing pain and guilt.

He'd lost everything when Natalie died, and now he was facing the same heartbreak all over again.

The fact that it wasn't his child didn't make a difference. It was Nychelle's child, and that made him or her special. Important.

He couldn't love a woman and not love her child.

And he loved Nychelle.

But he couldn't be with her, even if she wanted him to be. The terror pushing at him wouldn't allow it. The devastation he'd endured couldn't be repeated.

It would break him completely to go through it all again.

He'd felt the cracks opening in the armor keeping him safe as he'd listened to her. Her words had rendered him too broken to react—he'd barely been able to breathe. After she'd left the room he'd realized his hands were shaking, as though with ague. She'd been so upset by what he'd said, had looked so fragile as she'd walked into the bedroom, and his stomach twisted with anxiety as he thought of her being alone after she left.

He knew her independent streak, knew she wouldn't tell any of her family what had happened, and that spurred him to move.

Nychelle's handbag was on the floor, where it had fallen earlier, and he fished her phone out, glad to find she didn't have a lock code on it. He looked up her cousin's number, transferred it to his own phone, planning to call her once Nychelle had left. It was doubtful Nychelle would thank him for interfering, but there was no way he could watch her leave without knowing someone else would be checking on her.

He couldn't do it himself without falling apart.

When Aliya had said she would call Nychelle, and then, unable to contact her, that she'd be catching the first flight out of Atlanta, David had closed his eyes, fighting tears of thankfulness. Nychelle deserved to be taken care of right now, and he knew her parents wouldn't do it. They'd probably lecture her instead of nurturing her, and that was the last thing she needed.

Although he'd wanted to lecture her too—ask her why, with her medical problems, she'd taken a chance on getting pregnant. Didn't she know the heartbreak she was courting? Realize how devastating the loss of her child would be?

No. No. *No.*

He wouldn't think that—even as he feared it might happen. The baby would be fine. It had to be. She couldn't—wouldn't—go through the agony he'd experienced.

Gritting his teeth, he quickened his pace, even though his legs and lungs burned. Even as he prayed everything would work out for her, his anxiety built, growing to fill every nook and cranny of his soul.

"Stop it," he panted aloud. "Stop it!"

She would be all right. She had to be. The bright, beautiful light that shone in her eyes shouldn't be dimmed by that kind of pain. He couldn't bear to see that happen. Needed to force himself to believe everything would work out.

It was too hot to be running for this long. He knew he should turn back toward his car but he pressed on, the pain of overexertion a physical manifestation of his inner agony, tears mixing with the sweat running down his cheeks.

And when finally he collapsed on the sand, dragging air into his tortured lungs, there was only one thought left in his mind.

Despite everything, he wished he'd told her he loved her.

CHAPTER NINETEEN

NYCHELLE CHECKED THE blood pressure apparatus and, after jotting down the levels, smiled at her patient. “Everything looks good. You’re really doing well, Mr. Comstock.”

“Please—how many times do I have to ask you to call me Doug?” But he was smiling even as he groused.

“Doug,” she amended, returning his smile. “You’ve lost eighteen pounds in two months, which is amazing—but most important, your blood pressure is down.”

“Even better is the way I feel.” He was grinning now, obviously pleased with himself. “I’ve been sleeping like a baby, and I’m determined to drop the rest of the weight as soon as possible. I’ve been exercising like a fiend.”

“Just make sure you stick with the plan we worked out, okay? You want to make sure your nutritional needs are being met, and you don’t want to risk an injury, which could set you back.” Nychelle checked his chart again. “I see you have a follow-up appointment in a few weeks with Dr. Napoli, and that she diagnosed a herniated disc but deferred any treatment other than mild painkillers. Are you still having the leg pain?”

“It’s nowhere as bad.” Doug stretched out his legs and flexed his feet. “Dr. Warmington called that one, though, didn’t he? Both the diagnosis and Dr. Napoli not being willing to do much until I got my weight under control. Hey, where *is* the doc anyway?"

At the mention of David, Nychelle busied herself adding another note to the chart. "Usually I handle the follow-up appointments, but Dr. Warmington will be happy to see you if you particularly want his input."

"No, no—that's okay. I don't necessarily need to see him. I was just wondering if he was around."

Both disappointment and relief washed through her, and she kept her eyes on the tablet a moment longer than necessary, hoping Doug wouldn't see any of what she was feeling in her expression.

"Well, let's get going on these blood tests, so we can keep track of how your body is responding to the new regime."

Steering him away from talking about David worked for a while, but after they were finished, and Doug was getting ready to leave, he said, "I honestly think you and Dr. Warmington saved my life." He fussed with his collar, making it lie flat, while he spoke. "The two of you make a great team. If this place ever closes you should set up your own clinic somewhere. Believe me—just as I've been telling everyone I know in this neck of the woods to come to Lauderlakes, I'd be sending patients your way if you did."

"That's very kind of you," she said, and resolutely held her smile in place until she'd left him in the reception area to head back to her office. Then her happy expression fell away.

Doug had been her first patient of the day, and she was already wanting to go home. It had been a long couple of months, and just hearing David's name had the power to send a jolt of emotion through her. It was exhausting—especially considering how many times each week she either heard people talking about him or actually saw him. Hearing Doug praise the way they worked together made her remember David's hope to go back to South Carolina and open a practice. She'd actually imagined going with him, being an integral part of making his plan a reality.

That was her own pipe dream.

As she lowered herself into the chair behind her desk she sighed, wishing she'd had the courage to do what Aliya had suggested: talk to David about what had happened.

She'd meant to—she really had—but the first time she'd seen him at work after that fateful Saturday he'd given her a cool nod, his expression closed, unreadable. Frozen by that icy stare, she had felt her resolve shrivel up and die.

There was no way she could have braved a conversation with him under those conditions. And, although his attitude toward her didn't seem quite as bad anymore, there was still no evidence that beneath his distantly professional demeanor the David she'd fallen for still existed. Not even a hint that her behavior hadn't destroyed everything between them.

It still hurt terribly and, despite telling herself she needed to get over him, Nychelle's heart wasn't ready to listen to her head. Probably because her head wasn't actually fully on board with that concept yet either. Knowing she needed to move on wasn't the same as accepting it was time to do it.

Yet she'd promised herself she'd do the very best she could for her baby, no matter how she was feeling. Give him or her the very best chance. She needed to maintain a healthy emotional as well as physical balance, and doing so meant dealing with the reality of losing David.

It wasn't enough to cut back on her activities, like excusing herself from the free clinic planning committee. Although that, of course, had had the added benefit of eliminating one place where she'd see David while also allowing her the extra rest her body was demanding.

Who knew falling asleep could be so easy? It was as if when the baby decided it needed a nap, it involved Nychelle going to sleep too. Not an easy thing to deal with during her busy work days. Not to mention that many of her dreams, which were particularly vivid and included David, caused her to wake up either crying or sexually frustrated. Sometimes both. And her emotional mood swings were draining. Elation over the baby morphed seamlessly into desolation over David, leaving her almost shell-shocked at times.

Leaning back in her chair, she yawned as another wave of exhaustion washed through her. Rubbing her eyes, she thought maybe it was time to take another piece of Aliya's advice.

"You need some time off. Breathing room to get everything into perspective," Aliya had said. She'd insisted on video calling, since she wanted to see for herself how Nychelle was, and had always had the ability just to look at her cousin and know. "I'm sure you have some vacation time left."

She did. And now, as she reluctantly got up to go and greet her next patient, she made the decision to take a few days, maybe even a long weekend, to rest and get her head straight.

Clearing it with Human Resources wasn't as easy as she'd hoped, but she was able to take the following Friday as a personal day, plus the next Monday and Tuesday as vacation.

When she left the office on Thursday she was feeling lighter than she had in ages, determined to use her days off to concentrate on the baby. Nothing else. She already had plans on how she wanted to rearrange the house. It was time to put them into effect.

By the Monday afternoon of her vacation she was feeling both rested and accomplished. The hall cupboard, which was to become a small library, was cleaned out and ready for the organizer she'd ordered to be installed. Now she turned her attention to culling her books, which took up almost a full wall in the smallest of her three bedrooms—the room now used as an office, but soon to be the nursery. She assembled packing boxes for the books she planned to donate, and got down to it.

She'd just taped the last box closed when the doorbell rang.

"About time," she muttered, getting up off the floor. As the chimes pealed again, she called, "I'm coming." Adding, under her breath, "Impatient, much?"

She opened the door, expecting the shelving delivery man. Instead her heart leaped as she gazed up at the man standing outside.

"David."

His name was torn from a throat already closing in shock, coming out high and surprised. He didn't reply, or greet her, just stood there, his lips tight, his posture ramrod-straight. He looked leaner than usual, his face almost hawkish in its severity, and his hair was disheveled, as though he'd been running his fingers through it. When his gaze raked her from head to feet and back up again Nychelle's skin heated, tingled with awareness, and her heart seemed set to leap clear out of her chest, it was thumping so hard.

"Are you all right?"

It wasn't so much a question as a demand, shot at her like a bullet, making her jump.

"What? Yes." The words stuttered and stumbled from her lips.

"And the..." His gaze dipped again, only as far as her belly this time, and his jaw clenched an instant before he continued, "And the baby?"

"Fine," she replied softly, her heart aching. "We're both fine."

David exhaled, the breath leaving him in a *whoosh*, and he visibly sagged, reaching out to hold on to the doorjamb as though in need of its support.

"Thank God," he muttered, rubbing the back of his neck. *"Thank God."*

Stepping back, she asked, "Do you want to come in?"

He came through into the foyer, and instead of going into the living room stepped close and pulled her tight to his chest. As he buried his face in her hair Nychelle realized he was trembling, and instinctively wrapped her arms around his waist. Melting against him, inhaling his beloved scent, she allowed herself this moment, even though she didn't think the joy coursing through her veins would last.

"I was so worried about you."

It was a whisper against her temple. "Why?" she asked, just as softly.

"You weren't at work on Friday, and then again today. I thought..."

His voice faded and for an instant more she savored the sensation of being held so tenderly. Then she gently disengaged herself from his arms and stepped back.

David didn't try to stop her, just leaned against the wall and watched as she backed up far enough to perch on the arm of a chair. The door had swung shut, and in the quiet of the house they faced each other. She took a deep breath, trying to steady her heart, to be realistic, before she spoke.

"You thought I'd lost the baby?"

He nodded—just a single, staccato dip of his head, and she sighed.

"I just took a few days off. There was no need for you to worry. Besides, you could have just called or texted me before you got so upset."

The sound he made was indecipherable: a snort of what might have been interpreted as laughter, except there was no sign of amusement on his face. "You make it sound so simple."

"It *is* simple," she said, sad to think of having once more brought pain into his life.

Her heart ached to think of him suffering a moment more, even when she knew alleviating that hurt definitely meant them going their separate ways.

Lifting her chin, she looked straight into his eyes. "You need to stop torturing yourself because of my situation. You've dealt with enough without worrying about me. Just know that no matter what happens I'll be fine."

"And you're so rational," he said, as though she hadn't spoken, or as if he was offering commentary on a conversation that he wasn't really a part of. "Unfortunately there's no rationality left in me when it comes to you."

"David—"

Whatever she was planning to say was forestalled by his upheld hand.

"I need to explain."

He gave her a smile so sweet her heart melted.

"When I lost Natalie and my marriage fell apart, it made me question everything. What kind of doctor was I that I couldn't tell something was wrong? What kind of husband that my wife blamed me for her unhappiness both before and after we lost our baby? Had it been my fault Natalie was born too soon? It changed me in a fundamental way—made me fearful. Just the thought of going through something like that again made me lose all hope of having a family, of loving anyone again. Then I met you."

Nychelle could only stare at him, wondering if this were some kind of dream. David pushed away from the wall and paced closer, stopping about an arm's length away.

"I didn't want to get involved with you—fought it every step of the way. But you got under my skin and into my heart. It frightened me, made me want to run. And then…"

He faltered, and she saw him swallow before he went on.

"I hope you won't hate me for this, but when you told me about your medical problem I was elated. I saw it as a sign that we were meant to be together. We would grow our family through adoption, and I wouldn't have to worry about losing another child prematurely. Wouldn't have to risk my heart that way again. When you told me about the IUI I didn't know how to handle it. It didn't matter that it wasn't my child. It was yours, and I knew I would love your baby as if he or she were my own. I froze—was terrified."

Even as he said the words she could see his fear reflected in his eyes, in the tightness of his face, and her heart ached anew.

"It's okay," she whispered, wanting to put her arms around him again, comfort him, but knowing she shouldn't. If she did, she wouldn't want to let go. "I understand. I never meant to hurt you. I would have never done it on purpose."

The look he gave her was one of tenderness, and the softening of his face was so dramatic her heart leaped.

"Don't you think I know that?" He took another step closer, reached out to sweep a finger over her cheek. "You're the kindest, most amazing woman I've ever met. I know the last thing you'd want to do is hurt anyone. It's one of the things I love most about you."

He *loves* me?

He'd intimated it, but hearing it said so bluntly made her tremble, had tears welling in her eyes. Yet the barrier of his past still loomed between them, and although she'd love to ignore it, and pretend happily-ever-after was assured if they loved each other, she had to find the courage to face it head-on.

"David, you know there are no guarantees with this pregnancy." She searched his gaze, trying to gauge his reaction to her statement. "Look at how upset you were, thinking I might have lost the baby. And I still have such a long way to go. You don't need that kind of stress in your life and, believe me, I'll understand if you don't want to sign up for it."

Without breaking eye contact, David cupped her face, tilting it up toward his. She found her lips softening, longing blooming and spreading through her body. When his fingers settled, warm and strong on her skin, a little groan of need rose in her throat.

"I won't say it doesn't frighten me, but we'll get through it together." He caressed her lower lip with a sweep of one thumb. "I've allowed fear to rule my life too long. When we were apart I was consumed with wanting you, seeing you smile, hearing your voice, just being with you, and it was tearing me to pieces. I guess you could say my love for you is far stronger than my fears, and I'd rather be with you, no matter what, than try to exist without you."

"Suppose you change your mind?" she whispered, hope warring with her own fear to bring on a wave of insecurity. "What happens then?"

His smile was beautiful, open and happy. "You don't get it, do you? I'm yours—heart, body, mind and soul. Driving over here, half crazy with worry, I had to accept that I'll never be free from loving you. I thought if I just stayed away my feelings would fade, but now I know that will never happen."

His hands slipped from her face to her shoulders, urging her to stand. When she did, he wrapped his arms around her waist, but kept just enough space between them so they were face to face.

"I want to be the one who makes sure you're fine, no matter what. I want to be there for you every day, to hold your hand, or rub your feet, or tell you off when I think you're overdoing things. Say you love me again. Tell me you'll have me for the rest of our lives."

The love they shared washed over her, chasing away

her trepidation and filling her with joy. "Yes. Oh, David, I love you so much."

And then, enfolded in his arms, she lost herself in his kisses, completely secure for the first time in her life and exactly where she was supposed to be. All doubts cast aside.

EPILOGUE

"I WAS THINKING," David said, in a casual voice that Nychelle knew meant he was feeling anything but relaxed. "You should stop working soon."

This wasn't really a promising start to what she'd hoped would be a busy and productive Saturday. So many changes were coming, and coming so quickly her head sometimes felt as though it were spinning.

In less than eight weeks they'd welcome their baby, and as if that weren't enough they also had to sign the papers to purchase a practice close to David's home town. While he wouldn't take over from the retiring doctor there for another six months after that, Nychelle was determined to have as much dealt with on the home front as she could before the birth.

She had a to-do list as long as her arm, but David didn't seem inclined to go anywhere or do anything other than lie here. Or rather, he was probably inclined to have *her* lie there all day.

Lying across the bed, his head resting on her thigh, he rubbed her distended stomach, pausing every now and then to feel the baby turn or kick against his palm.

"Sweetheart, I'm just at thirty-two weeks," she replied. "And in good health. I don't want to stop working yet."

She'd been waiting for this to happen ever since she'd

had a scare at twenty-two weeks and her doctor had diagnosed placenta praevia. Dr. Miller was monitoring it carefully, and had scheduled Nychelle to have a Caesarian section five days before her due date, but David's stress levels had been climbing ever since. However, even though she wanted to alleviate his fears, knowing that she wouldn't be returning to Lauderlakes after the baby came made her want to maximize her earnings before she left. It was a *Catch 22.*

"I know," he answered, keeping his focus on her belly, his hand sliding around and around. "But it's something to think about."

Nychelle sighed, but made sure he didn't hear it. He'd been so good through her pregnancy up to this point—not hovering too much or allowing his doctoring instincts to take over; being concerned and engaged but not smothering.

Of course she knew he watched her when he thought she wasn't looking, and was sure he sometimes stayed awake at night to keep an eye on her when she wasn't feeling well. No matter what the doctor said, or how often she told David she was feeling wonderful, she knew he wouldn't really be okay until the baby was safely delivered.

She'd planned to work right up until the week before her C-section, but it looked like it was time for a compromise, and Nychelle carefully considered her words before saying them. "Well, why don't we—"

"Hang on," he said, his head coming up off her thigh. "Hold that thought."

He rolled to stand with a motion so fluid all she could feel was envy. The very last vestiges of grace had deserted her at least a month ago, and it often felt as though she needed a block and tackle to do the simplest things. Like get up out of a chair or push herself up to sit higher on her pillows.

Moments later he was back, carrying Jacqueline, who'd

just woken up. Like her mother, it took the toddler a while to face the day and become fully human again, and David was patting her back and joggling her gently, the way he knew she liked.

"Here we are," he said, placing a kiss on the top of Jackie's head. "Here's our beautiful girl, ready to rise and shine."

Nychelle chuckled when she caught sight of Jackie's expression. "Rise and shine" indeed. If the pout on their daughter's face was anything to go by, she had no intention of doing any such thing anytime soon.

"Mama," the little girl mumbled, reaching out with one arm while still keeping a tight grip on David's neck with the other.

Lowering himself and Jackie onto the bed with practiced ease, David lay down so the little body was snuggled between them.

"Good morning, my sweet girl," Nychelle said.

She was just reaching down to kiss Jackie's sleep-warmed cheek when the toddler abruptly sat up.

"Good morning, little bruvver," she said, in her scratchy, first-thing-in-the-morning voice, before leaning close to kiss Nychelle's tummy.

As Jackie flopped back down and rolled over, pulling at David's hand so he embraced them both, Nychelle knew a fullness of heart that never failed to make her eyes misty.

Looking across Jackie into her husband's beautiful blue eyes, she saw reflected there all she was feeling and more. And she smiled, knowing she was the luckiest woman alive.

"One more month," she said, moving her hand to cover his, which was back to circling her stomach. "Then I'll stay home."

"Two weeks," he said, as she'd expected.

"Three," she countered, her smile turning into a grin when he reluctantly nodded.

"Why do I feel as though that was what you'd decided

from the outset?" he grumbled, turning his hand to link his fingers with hers. "To you and Jackie I'm just a push-over, aren't I?"

She giggled, wrinkling her nose at him. "At least at the clinic you're still Dr. Heat, the man who has the nurses falling over themselves to do his bidding."

"Stop it," he growled, even as he swooped in to kiss the laughter from her lips. "Why can't I be Dr. Heat to *you* instead? I'd like that better."

"Oh, you are," she murmured against his mouth, surrounded in happiness, basking in the warmth of his love. "And you always will be."

* * * * *

MILLS & BOON

Coming next month

REUNITED WITH HER BROODING SURGEON

Emily Forbes

The gorgeous man with amazing bone structure stepped forwards and Grace's heart skipped a beat and her mouth dropped open.

Marcus Washington.

She could not believe it.

It had to be him. Even though he no longer resembled the twelve-year-old boy she once knew, it *had* to be him. There couldn't be two of him.

She hadn't thought about him for years but if she had she never would have imagined he would become a doctor. She knew that sounded harsh and judgemental but what she remembered of Marcus did not fit with her image of someone who had clearly ended up in a position of responsibility and service to others.

But what did she really know of him? She had only been seven years old. What had she known of anything?

Her father was a doctor and, at the age of seven, everything she knew or thought was influenced by what and who she saw around her. Particularly by her own family. And Marcus's family had been about as different from hers as a seven-year-old could have imagined. But she knew enough now to understand that it wasn't about where you came from or what opportunities you were handed in life, but about what you did with those opportunities, those chances. It was about the choices you made. The drive and the desire to be the best that you could be.

She would never have pictured Marcus as a doctor but now, here he was, standing in front of her looking polished, professional and perfect. It had to be him.

She knew a lot could change in twenty years and by the look of him, a lot had.

She was still staring at him, trying to make sense of what was happening when he looked in her direction and caught her eye. Grace blushed and, cursing her fair skin, the bane of a redhead, she looked away as his gaze continued on over her. She finally remembered to close her mouth.

Had he recognised her?

It didn't appear so, but then, why would he? She was nothing like the seven-year-old he had last seen.